Books should be returned or renewed by the last date above. Renew by phone **03000 41 31 31** or online *www.kent.gov.uk/libs*

7|15

Kent County Council
kent.gov.uk

Libraries Registration & Archives

CUSTOMER SERVICE EXCELLENCE

He dropped his gaze to take in her parted lips...lips he wasn't sure he could resist kissing.

Several times since they'd met they'd been this close, and each time he'd wanted nothing more than to lower his head and see precisely what it was that existed between them.

This time he wanted to follow through on that desire, and when he reached forward to tuck her hair behind her ear Cora's breath rushed out, as though she'd been holding it, waiting for him to make the first move.

'What is this?' he whispered, cupping her cheek with his hand, his thumb gently caressing her soft skin.

'I don't know.' She swallowed and placed her hands on his chest, gasping with delight at the contact. 'But I really want to find out.'

'So do I.'

With that, he lowered his head, desperate to finally get some answers.

Dear Reader

I love setting stories on my fictional island of Tarparnii. I can picture it quite clearly in my head and wish I could actually visit for real. Making up words and heritage for a fictional place is so much fun, and I guess that's one of the reasons why I like to revisit my Pacific Island Nation from time to time. This time around it's to introduce Cora—the second of the Wilton triplets—to Archer Wild.

Archer is such a dynamic hero it's little wonder that Cora falls in love with him. Likewise, Cora is everything Archer is looking for—even though he might take a while to realise it. Through it all, and drawing the characters closer together, is a gorgeous little boy: Nee-Ty. He has a cheeky smile and rarely walks anywhere, preferring to run as fast as his legs can carry him.

I do hope you enjoy getting to know Cora and Archer, as well as perhaps visiting some old friends: Daniel and Melora from DOCTOR: DIAMOND IN THE ROUGH. And keep an eye out for Molly Wilton's story—coming very soon!

With warmest regards

Lucy

A CHILD
TO BIND THEM

BY
LUCY CLARK

First published in Great Britain 2015
by Mills & Boon, an imprint of Harlequin (UK) Limited,
Large Print edition 2015
Eton House, 18-24 Paradise Road,
Richmond, Surrey, TW9 1SR

ISBN: 978-0-263-25490-7

Harlequin (UK) Limited's policy is to use papers that are natural, renewable and recyclable products and made from wood grown in sustainable forests. The logging and manufacturing processes conform to the legal environmental regulations of the country of origin.

Printed and bound in Great Britain
by CPI Antony Rowe, Chippenham, Wiltshire

Lucy Clark is actually a husband-and-wife writing team. They enjoy taking holidays with their children, during which they discuss and develop new ideas for their books using the fantastic Australian scenery. They use their daily walks to talk over characterisation and fine details of the wonderful stories they produce, and are avid movie buffs. They live on the edge of a popular wine district in South Australia with their two children, and enjoy spending family time together at weekends.

Recent titles by Lucy Clark:

These books are also available in eBook format from www.millsandboon.co.uk

DEDICATION

To my beautiful Melanie.
I adore you.
Love, Mum
Ps 3:3

Praise for
Lucy Clark:

'A sweet and fun romance about
second chances and second love.'
—*HarlequinJunkie* on
DARE SHE DREAM OF FOREVER?

CHAPTER ONE

'IS EVERYONE ACCOUNTED FOR?'

Cora Wilton leaned in closer towards her colleague, raising her voice above the gale-force winds surrounding them. Even though her hair was short, it didn't stop strands from whipping around into her face. She tucked them behind her ear and focused on watching Daniel's mouth so she could confirm what he was saying.

'Two people.' Daniel pointed behind her. 'Melora's bringing them in now.' As Cora turned, she saw Melora, Daniel's wife, helping two women; one elderly, the other about seventeen. The elderly woman was clearly distressed about something but Melora kept encouraging them to walk towards the large army trucks, which were the only way any of them were going to make it out of this area.

'What's she saying?' Daniel asked, unable to hear clearly as the wind whipped around them, drowning out what the elderly woman was saying in her native tongue of Tarparnese.

Cora had been working with Pacific Medical Aid on the Pacific island nation of Tarparnii for almost six months and as this was her second appointment with them, she was proud that she now understood quite a lot of the guttural dialect.

Cora crossed to the elderly woman's side as Melora helped the seventeen-year-old, who had bundles of blankets, clothes and other small possessions tied to her waist and shoulders in neat, organised rolls, and took the upset woman's hands in hers.

'I am listening to you,' Cora stated in Tarparnese. 'Please speak slower.'

The woman gripped Cora's hands and tried to slow her words and as Cora realised exactly what the woman was saying, her eyes widened in shock. 'Daniel!' Cora called, after placating the woman. 'She says her grandson is missing. His name is Nee-Ty and he's about three years old. No one can find him.'

Daniel came over and spoke more rapidly in his native tongue to the woman, gathering more information. 'She says the last time anyone saw him was almost half an hour ago. She sent the teenager to look for him but the girl couldn't find him.'

Cora walked over to the supplies, which were presently being bundled into large containers, ready to be loaded onto the truck. The evacuation of the village due to the oncoming storm was almost complete but there was no way she or any of her colleagues could live with themselves if they didn't take the time to search for the boy. She grabbed a two-way radio and handed the receiver to Daniel.

'Give me directions. I'll have a look.' Her colleague Melora grabbed another radio and tuned it in to Daniel's receiver.

'I'll go with you. It'll be faster if there are two of us searching.'

'All right,' Daniel said. 'We'll keep packing up here but that cyclone is only about twenty minutes away. You both know how quickly this tropical paradise changes into a nightmare so ten minutes is all you get. And if, for some reason, you don't make it back in time, head for the caves because we just can't wait around. The risk is too great. Agreed?'

'Agreed,' Cora and Melora said in unison. They turned and headed in the direction Daniel had told them.

'That poor little boy must be so scared.' Cora's voice was filled with concern.

'I know,' Melora agreed. 'My own children freak out whenever a storm passes over our house, let alone here in the jungle where the huts aren't exactly stable. Thank goodness they're on the other side of the island, safe and sound.'

They made their way through the deserted village, which had been stripped of as many possessions as people could carry. The native flowers growing outside some of the huts were already being torn to shreds by the increasing winds. Behind the village were small mountains that usually provided enough shelter but today they seemed very far away.

Cora had only been to this village once before during her time with PMA, but she'd been told there were large caves in the mountains where many years ago the villagers would have taken shelter from storms such as this one. Nowadays it was easier and safer to evacuate them, the loss of life far less than in years gone by.

Daniel called through on the radio to check on their progress but after three minutes of searching, Cora and Melora had to report they hadn't found him.

'Nee-Ty! Nee-Ty!' They called the boy's name over and over as Cora branched off in one direction and Melora another.

With the wind increasing, Cora soon needed the radio to talk to Melora, even though she couldn't be more than ten metres away. As she progressed further into the jungle-like scrub, some of the smaller trees almost bending double in the wind, Cora was having to continually brush her hair from her face in order to see. Ten minutes later, Daniel radioed that they both needed to come back.

'We can't wait any longer or we'll all be at risk.' She could hear the resignation in his voice at the decision he'd had to take, and she knew it wasn't an easy call for him to make.

'Copy that,' she said, after Melora had also radioed in that she was heading back.

As she turned to head back the way she'd come

Cora kept calling, kept hoping, kept praying that they would find the scared little boy.

'Nee-Ty! Nee-Ty!'

The sound from her mouth was being quashed by the wind, and as the howling sound of the approaching storm increased, visibility became an issue. She could barely see the track she'd used.

'Ooh.' She tripped on something and fell onto her hands and knees, dropping her radio in the process. Cora quickly searched for it but it didn't seem to be anywhere. 'This is bad, this is bad, this is bad,' she mumbled, as her heart rate increased, along with the approaching storm.

She continued to search on her hands and knees, the wind making it almost impossible for her to stand upright.

Panic began to worm its way into her mind and take hold. She was lost, in the jungle, with no radio and a fierce storm approaching. Yep. This was bad.

She thought about her sisters, Stacey and Molly; the three of them having been together since birth, the terrific trio. She thought about her younger siblings, Jasmine, George and Lydia, and how much she loved them. She thought of

Pierce, Stacey's new husband, and Nell, Pierce's sister, the two of them becoming as much a part of her life as the others. She loved them all. An unbidden sob escaped her lips and it was only then she realised she was working herself up into a tizz.

'That won't help you at all, Cora. Your family need you to be strong and get through this.' She spoke sternly to herself. 'You've been in difficult situations before. You love adventure. You're trained for situations like this...' She took a tentative step forward. 'Sort of...' she murmured.

Drawing a calming breath, she decided to leave the radio as searching for it would take away the precious minutes she now had at her disposal. Instead, she tried to view her situation objectively. She had to assume that her colleagues had done the right thing and left, getting all those other people to safety. They'd all had the same training as her and they knew she was more than equipped to look after herself. She would prove them right.

Daniel had mentioned the caves behind the village and at the moment heading towards them seemed like the logical course of action. Getting to a sheltered place was paramount. The rain would start to fall soon and the more ground she could cover before that happened, the better. Pushing her hair back from her face, she started off, constantly calling for Nee-Ty as she went.

Three times she stumbled but three times she picked herself back up and continued on, wishing she had lovely long hair like her sister Stacey so she could tie it back out of the way. Her sisters. Even thinking of them gave her strength to carry on. They wouldn't be at all impressed if their adventuring sister ended up being whisked away by a cyclone. She pressed on.

'Nee-Ty! Nee-Ty!' she continued to call as she pushed her way through the big tree leaves, the plantation surrounding her becoming more dense, the ground more rocky and uneven. The wind was becoming stronger, bending the large trees to and fro as though they were nothing but mere twigs. 'Nee-Ty!' It didn't matter that her words seemed to vanish into nothingness, she needed to try, needed to keep calling his name in the hope that he, too, had started heading this way.

Would a three-year-old know to do that? Would

his instincts help him to seek shelter? She knew the children on Tarparnii were educated in the ways of the land first and foremost before any formal education such as learning to read and write was even considered. Had Nee-Ty been taught these things by the village elders, by the people who cared for him, by the other children he would have played with? She prayed it was so.

As the wind increased, so did the slope of the land and soon she was using both hands to climb over the boulders jutting out from the base of the mountain. The wind wasn't as fierce here due to the small shelter the rocks on her left provided. She was also thankful that it wasn't raining yet as it would make this climb ten times more difficult. She pulled herself up onto a small ledge, crouched down and flattened herself against the rock, turning to look back the way she had come. The evacuated village was being attacked by the full force of the wind and as she watched, a thatched roof lifted off one of the huts and was whisked away.

She shook her head in awe at the power of Mother Nature whilst she felt pain for the people whose homes were being destroyed at the mercy of the weather. And what of little Nee-Ty? Wherever he was, he must be so incredibly frightened. She cupped her hands around her mouth and yelled with all her might. 'Nee-Ty!'

'Ni-Kaowa!'

Cora was startled at receiving a reply. She swung around, positive the sound had come from not too far behind her. 'Nee-Ty,' she called again, and once more received the same reply.

'Ni-Kaowa!'

Cora gasped with delight at hearing his reply, her tired and aching limbs once more invigorated with renewed energy. Quickly and carefully, she scrambled over the ledge, calling again, pleased when the reply came once more but this time the voice was nearer. She spoke in Tarparnese, telling him to stay where he was but to keep calling out to her. When he did, the elation Cora felt at having actually found the little boy filled her with such a sense of happiness she had to stop herself from crying tears of relief. It wouldn't do for her vision to be blurred right now, not when she was trying to climb rocks. Nee-Ty needed her and she needed him. How he'd managed to climb up this far, she had no idea, but at least he was safe.

'Nee-Ty?'

'Ni-Kaowa.'

He was right around the next bend and a moment later she saw him. Hoisting herself up to another tiny ledge, she instantly gathered the little boy up into her arms and held him tight. He didn't seem to have any hesitation in accepting her embrace, especially as she murmured over and over again, 'I've got you. It's OK. I've got you.' Her words were a mixture of English and Tarparnese but Nee-Ty didn't seem to care, he understood the sentiment.

Cora sat back on the ledge, resting her back against a rock, Nee-Ty in her arms, as she wondered what on earth she was supposed to do next. She breathed in and could smell the rain. The two of them would be drenched in a matter of minutes. She knew they had to move, had to find the caves Daniel had mentioned, but she had no idea where they might be. She tried asking Nee-Ty if he knew where the caves were but all he did was bury himself further into her arms, shaking with fright at the increase of the howling winds.

She needed to stand, to make her way around the next corner to search for a cave but whenever she tried to move, Nee-Ty clung to her. There was no way she'd be able to carry him and search for the cave in these conditions but she had to. Perhaps she could put him on her back, trusting that his survival instinct would help him to hold on tight, but…

The sound of an engine revving startled her and she turned her head to the right, her eyes anxiously scanning the scrub land beneath her. The trees seemed to be bending, making way for something that was quite large and powerful. Cora's eyes widened when she caught her first glimpse of the largest truck she'd ever seen, complete with a large metal shovel on the front, ploughing its way through with force. It was also headed towards the base of the mountain. And when the truck finally reached its destination, a man dressed in fatigues sprang from the driver's side, a pack on his back, before scrambling up the boulders with ease. Those same boulders had sapped most of Cora's breath and strength and yet she could see him tackling them as though he were a mountain goat.

Was she seeing things? She blinked rapidly a few times but the image remained. Who was he and what was he doing here?

She realised the answers to her unspoken questions didn't really matter. The fact was that he was headed her way. She didn't care whether or not he'd specifically come looking for them or was himself trying to get to somewhere more sheltered before the tropical cyclone unleashed its fury on them.

'Hey! Hey! Over here!' she called, her voice becoming hoarse from all the yelling she'd been doing. Still, she kept on trying to get his attention, hoping her words weren't disappearing with the wind and that he would actually realise there were other people up here.

'Hello. We're over here.' Her voice cracked and she tried to swallow over her sore throat.

'I can hear you. Keep calling to me.' His voice was deep, firm and British, and a lot closer than she'd anticipated, but Cora instantly did as she was told. Within half a minute he was scrambling up onto the ledge beside her. He crouched down and reached out a hand, his fingers gently brushing her hair from her eyes. 'Dr Wilton, I presume,' he remarked.

'Y-yes.' Cora wasn't sure why she stammered, whether from the relief at being rescued or from his tender touch, but either way she was relieved at having been found. As he knew her name, it was clear he'd been sent to find her. How he had tracked her down she didn't know, neither did she care. 'I was trying to find the caves. I don't know where they are.'

'I do,' he replied, and within another instant he helped her to her feet and took the clinging Nee-Ty into his big strong arms. He murmured to the boy in fluent Tarparnese, reassuring him and telling him they were going to the caves and safety. Not giving Nee-Ty the chance to respond, the man led the way, telling Cora to follow exactly in his footsteps.

'Just make sure you don't take steps that are too long,' she returned.

'As you wish.' His rounded English words made her heart skip a beat but she quickly quashed the sensation. Now was not the time to be enthralled by his voice, or by his broad shoulders, or his long legs, or his heroic demeanour. They needed to focus, to move, to get to safety as soon as possible.

With that, they set off, the pace far brisker then she was comfortable with, but he seemed to know where they were headed and at the moment Cora had no other option but to put her complete trust in him. When the rain began, he went even faster, but his movements were still sure-footed.

'Almost there,' he called, his words muffled by the wind and rain. They were all drenched within a matter of seconds, the punishing rain stinging her skin.

'We just need to jump over this small gap to that ledge over there,' he remarked, turning to slide his free arm around her waist. Before Cora could even understand what he was saying, she felt herself being picked up and held close to her rescuer, Nee-Ty secure in his other arm. He took two fast steps almost as a run-up and in the next instant they'd made it safely across the gap.

'Who *are* you? A superhero?' Cora's question was asked more out of disbelief rather than curiosity. He didn't release her but instead continued to carry her a few steps further until they entered the entrance to a cave.

'There you are, Dr Wilton.' He set her to the ground, not releasing his hold on her waist until he was sure her legs could support her. His words were louder, echoing around the stone walls, no longer having to fight with the stormy elements outside.

Cora opened her mouth to thank him but nothing came out. He didn't seem too perturbed by anything that was happening as he continued to make his way further into the darkness of the cave. He rummaged through one of the many pockets in his trousers and a second later pulled out a torch. He shone it around the area.

'Not the most shiny cave in the world but it will definitely serve its purpose.'

Again when Cora tried to talk she found her voice robbed of sound. Instead, her teeth began to chatter as the wetness from her clothes starting to seep in.

'Keep moving, Dr Wilton. A little further in and then you can collapse.'

Cora nodded and followed his steps, glancing at Nee-Ty, who looked incredibly tiny in their rescuer's arms. The little boy had his hands firmly around the man's neck as though he was never letting go. This was confirmed when they finally came to a stop and the man tried to release Nee-Ty.

'The child appears to be glued to me.' He turned to face Cora. 'Dr Wilton, if you would be so kind as to take the boy, I have blankets and other provisions we'll be needing in my pack.'

Cora dutifully held out her hands to the boy and with a hint of reluctance Nee-Ty went to her. She sat down on the cold stone and dirt ground, cuddling Nee-Ty close to her, both for warmth and reassurance.

'Excellent.' The man took his pack off and started taking equipment out, one of the first things being a space blanket, which he placed over Cora and Nee-Ty. 'There you are. Stay warm while I get things organised.'

Again Cora watched him in a state of disbelief as he moved with purpose and focus. 'Wh-what about y-you?' Her voice was hoarse and her teeth were chattering. 'Aren't y-you c-cold?'

He stared at her for a brief moment before returning his attention to his task. 'I've been through far worse than this.' The earlier strong winds had blown quite a bit of debris into the opening of the cave and after a brief 'I'll be back' her rescuer disappeared, thoughtfully leaving the torch nearby, illuminating the area.

Ordinarily, Cora would have wanted to take a closer look at her new surroundings, wanting to investigate, to see whether they shared this cave with any other creatures who might also be sheltering from the storm, but exhaustion was beginning to catch up with her. She shifted a little so she could lean against the wall, needing to rest her head. She tightened her arms around Nee-Ty, who was more than happy to snuggle close. Her eyelids were just too heavy.

The memory came of the man's arms, sliding about her, drawing her close, before he'd jumped across that gap in the rocks, the way his firm torso had felt against hers, the way she'd placed her hand around his neck, the broad shoulders making her fingers look small. Her mind replayed the event, slowing down the moments, which had passed all too fast. Who was this man?

Just another volunteer were the words he

seemed to speak in her dream. Then Cora felt her toes beginning to thaw out and her body temperature begin to return to normal. Her clothes were drying somehow and her head was resting on something comfortable. She couldn't remember ever feeling this content in her life and as she turned and snuggled closer, vaguely aware of a child lying next to her, Cora gave herself up to her dreams, especially as they contained vivid images of her tall, dark and handsome rescuer.

You're amazing, she whispered softly to him.

Thank you, he returned, the words a little clipped, as though he was uncomfortable receiving the compliment. *Sleep, Dr Wilton. I'll protect you.*

Always?

Silence surrounded her but a band of firm warmth tightened around her shoulders. Sighing, she relaxed completely, feeling…quite content.

CHAPTER TWO

WHEN SHE AWOKE the next morning, Cora found it difficult to open her eyes, instead preferring to stay still a moment longer, trying to hang on to her wonderful dream. A tall, dark and handsome man had rescued her. His scent had been one of rain, sweat and the slightest hint of spice, but the warmth he'd exuded had wrapped around her like a comfortable, secure blanket. She sighed, a small smile tugging at the corners of her mouth. 'Nice,' she murmured, the word echoing around her.

Echoing?

The thought was enough to snap her mind to attention and she sat bolt upright, her eyes wide as she took in her surroundings, the events of the previous day flooding back with force. 'Nee-Ty!' The little boy's name was a startled whisper upon her lips. The realisation that he was no-where in sight propelled her to her feet. She was in a cave. Her own personal superhero had rescued her...a man who bore an exact resemblance to the man she'd just been dreaming about. She shook her head. Now was not the time to rehash those exciting dreams. She had to find Nee-Ty.

There were charred remnants of a fire near her feet, which she realised *he* had made. His backpack was still there, leaning up against the wall of the cave, so he couldn't be too far away. She just hoped Nee-Ty hadn't run away again but was instead safe with their rescuer.

'Nee-Ty?' she called, her voice catching on the words as she belated realised just how dry her throat was. She tried to swallow but it only seemed to make matters worse. All the yelling she'd done yesterday as the cyclone had approached, as she'd tried to find Nee-Ty, had taken its toll on her vocal cords.

Stumbling to the front of the cave, she raised a hand to shield her eyes from the bright sunlight, squinting as she looked around for any signs of Nee-Ty and her rescuer. Instead, she gasped at the devastation before her. Where the village had been there was only trees, rubble and debris. Most of the huts had been torn to shreds and the gardens where fresh vegetables and flowers had grown were no more. Such had been the force of the cyclone that even the large vehicle her superhero had used had been tipped onto its side. Cora shook her head. If they hadn't made it safely to the cave… She shuddered at the thought. But they *had* made it to safety, thanks to *him*.

She heard a sound just to her left and spun in that direction, her gaze frantically scanning the area, her heart rate increasing. Was it an animal or was it them? She held her breath, listening intently to any little sound. Tarparnii had some very different kinds of native animals and a few of them were the kind that you really didn't want to cross paths with, especially if they were looking for food after such a storm.

When she heard chatter in Tarparnese, she placed a hand over her heart and breathed a sigh of relief. There were two male voices, one young and one extremely deep and extremely sexy, heading her way. Before Cora could move, they rounded the bend and she couldn't help but smile at the sight of Nee-Ty on the man's back, his little arms holding on tight to those firm, broad shoulders.

The man's steps were confident as he came up the small incline that led to the cave mouth. It was her first real opportunity to see him in the light of day without the effects of a storm lashing around her, and as he hadn't yet seen her standing there, she didn't feel too self-conscious giving him the once-over. Her sister, Molly, would have been so proud of her.

He had dark hair, cut in the military style of short back and sides. His movements were structured yet fluid and natural. The dark green fabric of his fatigues pulled taut across his thighs as he moved and his feet were enclosed in a pair of black army boots. Everything about him yelled 'military man' but she knew the British military had ceased their peacekeeping missions in Tarparnii many years ago.

He answered a question Nee-Ty had asked but his words faltered for a split second when he saw her standing there, watching them. 'Dr Wilton. You're finally awake.'

She raised an eyebrow at the 'finally'. 'I didn't realise I was supposed to set an alarm.' She kept her smile in place as he walked past her.

'No need for an alarm.' He immediately lifted

Nee-Ty from his back with ease then raised the leather cover from the watch on his wrist. 'We're still ahead of schedule.'

Cora frowned. Didn't he realise she'd been joking? She knew sometimes her relaxed Australian humour didn't necessarily translate well to the Tarparnese people but surely, being British, he should have known she hadn't been serious. She shook the thought from her head and focused on Nee-Ty, who was jumping up and down, clearly excited about something, repeating his words over and over.

'Berries. We got berries,' he said in Tarparnese. 'I know where they are. Berries.' He was pointing to the man's trousers and Cora wasn't at all sure what he meant until the man pulled a bag from one of his many pockets and held up the berries.

'Nee-Ty knew exactly where to look.' He nodded at the little boy, clearly impressed at the three-year-old's knowledge of the area. 'The bush was tucked away in between two boulders and therefore sheltered from the overpowering elements of the storm.'

'I picked them. I did it. It is my job and I did

it.' Nee-Ty was still jumping around in excitement, pointing at the man. '*He* did it at the top.'

'That is correct,' the man clarified, speaking in the native tongue. 'Nee-Ty picked the ones lower down and I picked the ones at the top.' He looked at the boy. 'Excellent teamwork.' He nodded once to the boy and was utterly astonished when Nee-Ty ran towards him, hugging his legs. He froze for a moment then placed a tentative hand on the boy's head and patted it twice. 'A job well done.' He looked as though he was about to say something else but decided against it. Instead, he stepped back, breaking the contact. Nee-Ty stared up at him for a moment, the happiness sliding from his face as though he was waiting to be told off.

Cora's heart turned over with sympathy for the boy and she quickly crouched down and opened her arms to him. 'Tell me again how you picked the berries.' She swallowed over her scratchy throat, ignoring the feeling as the little boy ran into her open arms.

'I did not break them. I was good. I did it.' While Nee-Ty's delight returned to his eyes as he sat with Cora, she watched as her English hero pulled some other bits and pieces from his backpack.

He seemed to know exactly what he was doing and apparently they had a schedule to maintain. Cora watched his movements, sure and steadfast. It was natural that all of her senses were heightened, she'd just come through a life-threatening situation and *he* had been the one to—literally—save her life. Of course she was grateful to him, of course she was going to view him with some level of hero-worship. But she also knew that he was just a man, one who had used his skills to help others. She frowned a little, her logical thought processes doing nothing to stop her heart from racing when he glanced her way.

He pulled a few silver food sachets from his backpack and held them up. 'The fresh berries will go nicely with the freeze-dried cereal rations.'

Cora opened her mouth to thank him, but no sound came out. She quickly swallowed, trying not to grimace at the soreness of her throat. She waited a moment and tried again, noticing that he was watching her closely, a hint of concern on his brow. 'Are the berries safe enough to eat?'

'Nee-Ty ate them and told me he has them every morning. His grandmother would send him and some of the other children out to pick them.' There was the smallest hint of sadness in his words as they acknowledged that Nee-Ty's little world had dramatically changed overnight.

'Surely she hadn't sent him out yesterday to pick them, knowing there was a storm coming?'

'No. She had told him to stay close to the camp but then he told me that some other bigger kids had told him to go and pick berries.' He frowned. 'He was excited because they usually didn't let him pick them because he squashed them.'

Cora's eyes widened in shock and her arms tightened around the little boy, who was still smiling, watching the conversation between the two adults, completely oblivious to what they were discussing. She swallowed before speaking. 'They can't have sent him away from the village on purpose, can they?'

She had no idea how much English the child understood but perhaps now was not the time to discuss this topic. She met the man's gaze, amazed at how he seemed to be communicating the same silent message to her. *Let it go... for now.*

Cora nodded and pointed to the rations he still held in his hand. 'Looks as though we're in for a morning feast.' Her Tarparnese words were delivered via a hoarse whisper but there was a bright smile on her face as she looked at Nee-Ty. 'A morning feast and perhaps some introductions?' She looked pointedly at her rescuer. 'I still don't know your name.'

He cleared his throat and nodded. 'Of course. A slight oversight. Names weren't high on the list when we first met.'

'No.' She grinned, agreeing with him. 'There were a few other thing that required attending to.'

'Exactly.'

'Such as...not dying.' Cora chuckled as he shifted the freeze-dried packs to his left hand and held out his right towards her.

'Archer.'

'Archer,' she repeated, unsure whether that was his first name, last name or nickname. Her small hand was enveloped in his warm one. The shake he gave was firm, precise and over in an instant, yet the warmth from the brief touch seemed to travel up her arm, causing a burst of sensual awareness to flood her body. Cora immediately wrapped both arms around Nee-Ty, giving her shoulders a little shake in order to dispel the sensation.

'I'd like to take a look at your throat, just to make sure you haven't done any real damage.'

'You're a doctor?' Now that did surprise her, even though she hadn't really given any thought to his occupation, other than that of rescuer.

'Yes.' He raised one eyebrow as though he was intrigued by her surprise. Cora wished he hadn't because that simple action had brought forth another wave of awareness, his blue eyes watching her intently. Archer was having a devastating effect on her equilibrium and right now she needed to be as clear headed and as focused as possible. The way he was making her feel was nothing more than a delayed reaction of gratitude for everything he'd already done for her.

'So...uh...' She cleared her throat again, trying not to wince in pain. 'What's the plan?'

'Right. First...' He turned from staring at her and dug around in his backpack, pulling out a canteen of water. 'Have a drink in order to lubricate your vocal cords.'

Cora accepted the water bottle from him, unscrewed the lid and took a grateful sip. She had an intense desire to glug the entire contents of the bottle, but she resisted the urge, knowing that little sips would do her body far more good than sloshing around with too much water.

'Then I'll check your throat. We'll eat, pack up camp, then make our way down to the mountain. We're due to rendezvous with our rescue party in just over an hour.'

'You managed to get a call through?'

Archer patted one of the pockets in his trousers. 'Satellite phone was still working. They're thrilled we're all safe. Daniel and Melora were beside themselves with worry, not only for Nee-Ty but for you. Daniel knew I was in the vicinity with the road-maker—uh, that's what we call the truck I was driving.'

'You mean the one currently tipped onto its side?'

He nodded as though totally impressed with the position of his truck. 'Those winds were a mite strong. At any rate...' He shook his head and continued with his preparations as he spoke. 'When they were forced to leave without you, Daniel put out the call. I answered and told him I'd plough my way through towards the caves to see what I could find.'

'It was a long shot.'

'It was an adventure.' Archer's blue eyes twinkled with a look she knew all too well. It was the look of an adrenaline junkie and she had to admit that it only enhanced his already handsome features. 'Granted, a fairly calculated one,' he continued. 'I'd caught a glimpse of you climbing the boulders as I drove in, so at least I had a direction in which to head.'

'That was fortunate.'

'It was. If the rain had been coming down by then, I never would have spotted you. As it was, we *did* manage to rendezvous and now my good friend Daniel is very relieved. He mentioned that he hadn't fancied having to tell your family any bad news.'

Cora nodded, thinking quickly. 'I'll have to try and contact my sister as soon as possible. Once Stacey hears about the cyclone passing over Tarparnii, she'll be on instant stressed-out alert.'

'Your sister?'

'Yes. She's a worrier.'

'Right.' Archer glanced at her once more before he continued preparing their morning feast. 'I'd just presumed Daniel was referring to your husband.'

'My husband?' Cora shook her head. 'I don't have a husband.' And she probably never would because once men found out she had...certain problems, she instantly became repulsive to them. She looked away and closed her eyes for a second, determined not to think about her past hurts. Usually she was pretty good but for some reason, any time anyone presumed she was married or was surprised she didn't have a husband, it brought those old wounds to the surface and rubbed salt in them.

'Are you all right?'

Cora opened her eyes to find Archer kneeling in front of her, a tongue depressor and penlight torch in his hands. Nee-Ty started squirming in her hands and she instantly let him go. He headed over to the bag with the berries and instantly started munching on them.

She swallowed, her throat still scratchy. 'Fine.'

He nodded as though he didn't believe her in the slightest but thankfully didn't pursue the matter. 'Let's get this check-up done so we can eat and stay on schedule.' Archer's words were still brisk and to the point yet Cora could have sworn she detected the smallest hint of concern in his tone. Was he concerned about her throat or something else?

'Stick out your tongue and say "Ahh".'

Cora did as she was told and after a moment of looking at her throat Archer withdrew the tongue depressor.

'Just a little red. I have some chewing gum you can have after breakfast in order to assist with keeping your throat lubricated.'

'OK. Thanks.' He was close. So close she could smell that spicy scent that she recalled had surrounded him yesterday. It was nice. Soothing. Comforting. She continued to stare into his eyes, eyes that no longer twinkled with adrenaline delight but rather seemed to be trying to figure her out.

Cora swallowed, trying not to grimace as she did so. Archer's closeness was starting to unnerve her, especially when his gaze dipped from her eyes to take in her slightly parted lips. 'Drink some more water,' he instructed before clearing his own throat and turning away.

She looked down at the canteen next to her and went through the motions of taking a sip, trying not to watch every move Archer made. He handed Nee-Ty the first freeze-dried pack of rations mixed with fresh berries, and the little boy tucked into it with the ravenous hunger of a mountain lion.

'So…' Her voice cracked again and she took another sip from the water bottle. 'Uh…do you know Daniel well?'

'Very well,' he replied. 'Daniel and I were at school together.'

'Wow. So that's a long time.'

'It is. I was coming to Tarparnii to spend my holidays here long before I ever realised I'd one day be working with PMA.'

'Hence why you seem to speak the language far more fluently than me.'

Archer shrugged before handing her the next rations packet. She accepted it with thanks, ensuring their fingers didn't touch as the last thing she needed right now was to feel that confusing warmth spread through her once again.

'There are no spoons. Sorry.'

'It's fine.'

She knew their present situation was rather intimate but once they were back with the rest of their team, doing their work, these moments would be nothing more than small memories. The awareness of his pure masculine presence would dissipate and her thoughts would once more become structured, ordered and focused on the job she'd come here to do. Maintaining a level of professionalism would surely help in this situation and the first thing she needed to do was to thank him for rescuing her. As her father had always taught her and her siblings, there was never any excuse for bad manners.

'Mmm. Not bad,' she remarked after taking the first mouthful and only then realising just how hungry she was.

'It serves its purpose,' he agreed.

Cora swallowed then looked across at him. 'Thank you, Archer.'

'For…breakfast? You're welcome.'

'No. No, I mean thank you for rescuing me.'

He seemed unnerved by her words and shifted a little but she wasn't going to let his discomfort stop her from thanking him properly.

'You saved my life. Mine and Nee-Ty's.' She held his gaze, her words heartfelt and intent. *'Thank you.'*

Archer didn't look away but instead nodded once. 'You're very welcome, Cora.' There was no jest or awkwardness to his words, his tone one of quiet sincerity. For a whole five seconds they simply stared at each other before Archer broke the moment by picking up his breakfast portion and starting to eat.

A few hours later they'd managed to climb down from the cave onto solid ground, but picking their way through the debris left by the tropical cyclone took time. Nee-Ty was quite nimble and fast at scrambling over things, especially as he wore no shoes, but at times he required help. He was light enough that Cora could carry him on her back for a bit and at one point she even she managed to coax Archer into putting the little boy onto his shoulders.

'He's as light as a feather,' she rationalised. 'And he has good balance.' She was sure Archer only agreed to ensure they met their rendezvous. Seeing him carry Nee-Ty reminded her of the way her father had carried her when she'd been little. She'd felt as though she could conquer anything when she'd been on her daddy's shoulders, as though nothing in the world could ever go wrong. How quickly she'd learned otherwise.

Nee-Ty pushed some of the higher leaves out of Archer's way as the man's long legs strode purposefully forward, the pack on his back and the boy on his shoulders. 'He's actually quite helpful.' The words seemed to be delivered with a hint of surprise.

'You are a champion,' she told Nee-Ty in Tarparnese, and the little boy laughed and pumped his fists in the air like he'd just won a marathon. Cora smiled at the boy and clapped her hands with delight. She was also trying to distract herself from looking at the way the material from Archer's cotton shirt pulled across his broad shoulders. Instead, she should be concentrating on where she was putting her feet, because the last thing they needed at the moment was for her to lose her focus and to slip, fall and sprain her ankle.

'Whoa. Do not move around too much,' Archer told the boy. Nee-Ty's smile slipped from his face before he immediately placed his hands on Archer's head and sat as still as possible.

Cora considered Nee-Ty's behaviour, wondering what sort of life the little boy had had because if it hadn't been a happy one, it was probably going to get worse once he saw the village. Her heart went out to him and she vowed to do anything she could in order to support the child and reunite him with the rest of his family.

It wasn't long before Nee-Ty began wriggling, saying he wanted to get down, and Archer stopped, lifting the boy from his shoulders with ease. Again Cora found her gaze drawn to those firm, sculpted arms of his. It wasn't that she was leering at him but rather…appreciating the way he moved.

'It is time to sit now,' Nee-Ty told both the adults, and pointed up at the sky, as though to indicate that the sun was also telling them to rest. It was starting to get warm and Cora was more than happy to follow Nee-Ty's lead.

Where the little boy had stopped was near a group of trees that were half-uprooted but were somehow leaning on each other, creating a natural canopy. 'Perfect.' Archer took off his pack and gathered some of the larger fallen leaves and placed them on a patch of smoothish ground beneath the canopy. 'There you are, Cora. Should be a bit more comfortable for you.'

Surprised at his thoughtfulness, Cora smiled. 'Well, thank you, my superhero.'

'Please, don't call me that.' His words came out in a rush and once they were said he instantly clenched his jaw as though immediately regretting it.

Cora's smile slipped as she sat down. 'Oh. I'm sorry. I didn't mean anything by it. I was...' she shrugged '...only joking.'

Archer stood there, his hands low on his hips, looking down at her for a moment as though he regretted saying anything. He exhaled harshly then sat down near her.

'It's just that...' He stopped again, raking a hand through his hair, clearly uncomfortable. 'Such a label...' He clenched his jaw but held her gaze. 'It makes me feel as though I have to live up to expectations when I'm not really any type of superhero. I'm just a man.'

Cora watched the nonchalant shrug of his shoulders, the way he seemed incredibly uncomfortable talking about anything remotely personal. Nee-Ty shuffled closer to her and Cora instantly drew him nearer, dropping a kiss to his head. 'Have a rest, sweetie,' she crooned, and even though she spoke in English, Nee-Ty seemed to understand her words as he rested his head on her knee.

'I didn't mean to make you feel—'

'I know.' He rubbed his fingers on his forehead. 'Look, forget I said anything.'

'No. You have a right to speak up, Archer. It's OK.' She smiled at him and although he might not want her calling him that, it didn't mean she'd stop thinking about him in such a way. He'd appeared out of nowhere, swooped down to pick her up and carried her to safety.

He dropped his hand and nodded, then turned and opened his pack, pulling out some more rations of water and freeze-dried food. 'You're very natural with children,' Archer eventually remarked.

Cora nodded as she took a sip of water. Nee-Ty was now sleeping soundly so she passed the canteen back to Archer. 'I have a lot of siblings.'

'A lot? How many quantifies "a lot"?'

'Five.'

'Five! Wow. That is a lot of siblings,' he remarked, mulling over this information.

'How about you? Any siblings?'

His jaw clenched again as though he was trying to stop himself from saying something. He shook his head. 'I'm an only child. I went to boarding school, then military school, then medical school.'

'Wow. That is a lot of schooling.' She couldn't resist teasing him a little, and when Archer smiled, Cora felt her heart skip a beat. Did the man have any clue just how dynamic his smile was? She found it difficult to look away, her own smile increasing as she allowed a new wave of sensations to wash over her, sensations of awareness of just how handsome the man in front of her was.

'So, these siblings you have, I take it you're all close?' he asked, bringing her convoluted thoughts back to the present.

Cora nodded. 'Closer than you'd think. I have two younger sisters and a younger brother but Stacey, Molly and I are one of three.'

'Three? As in you're triplets?' He seemed stunned and amazed, as did most people when they met triplets.

'Yes. I'm the middle one. Stacey is five minutes older, Molly is five minutes younger and we're not identical.'

Archer looked at her with incredulity. 'You've never been alone. Your entire life.'

'Nope. Even out here, I usually manage to talk to them a few times a week.'

'Via internet chat?'

'Yes, or satellite phone.'

Archer reached down into one of his many trouser pockets and pulled out his satellite phone. He checked the reception on it, nodding in approval before handing it to her. 'Here. You said you wanted to reassure your sister. Call her now. I'm sure she'll have heard about the cyclone hitting Tarparnii, which means she's going to want to know you're OK.'

'Really?' Cora reached out to take the phone from him, careful not to disturb Nee-Ty. 'Thank you, Archer. That was, of course, at the back of my mind and the sooner I can get word to them, the better.'

'Then by all means, Dr Wilton, dial away.'

Cora eyes widened with delight as she pressed the buttons, not even stopping to calculate the time difference between the two countries, knowing there would be no way Stacey would be sleeping until she was sure her sister was OK. Proof of this was when Stacey answered on the first ring.

'Hello? Hello?'

Cora could hear the urgency in her sister's voice and it gave her great joy to dispel it.

'Stace. It's me. I'm fine.'

'Oh, Cora. Thank goodness. We've been listening to the news on the radio and watching the internet for updates but—'

'I'm fine, Stace.'

'Molly knew you were. She's been telling me to chillax and rely on the "bond". You know how she gets. When the situation gets stressful—'

'Molly becomes super-calm. Like a leaf…on the wind,' Cora replied with a smile. 'Listen,

Stace, I can't talk now. I just wanted to let you know I'm OK.'

'Thanks. Love you, sis.'

'Love you all, too.' Cora disconnected the call and handed the phone back to Archer, knowing he'd been sitting close enough to hear both sides of the conversation. 'Thank you.' She sighed with a warm happiness that only her family could give her. 'I feel so much better now.'

'You do? How?'

Cora frowned for a second, wondering if he was winding her up.

'I have no siblings, remember? You look so… content, relieved. How does this happen?'

'Oh. I've never really thought about it.' She scratched the side of her head as she thought. 'Well, just hearing Stacey's voice, knowing I was able to dispel her fears, to give her peace of mind was good.' She placed a hand to her chest. 'It makes me feel good knowing I can do that for her.'

'Anything else?'

'Oh. OK, well, I guess it feels comforting and calming.'

Archer nodded then angled his head to the

side. 'Does it feel good knowing someone else is worrying about you?'

She thought on that. 'I guess so. Makes me feel very loved. And now, thanks to you allowing me to use your phone, my siblings can sleep well, knowing I'm safe.'

Archer didn't respond to her words right away. Instead, he drew in a deep and calming breath, slowly letting it out. 'It must be nice.' There was a hint of jealousy combined with longing in his tone. 'Having people care about you.' He tucked the phone back into his pocket.

'You don't have anyone to call?'

'No.'

'What about your parents?'

'My mother died when I was ten and my father passed away last year.' And he'd been hounded by his father's company advisers to return to England and to take his rightful place as heir of the Wild Corporation. It was the last thing he ever wanted to do. Conglomerates and the aristocracy were the last places he would ever choose. He'd rather brave a cyclone than put on a suit and work from nine to five.

'I'm sorry to hear that.' She was aware that his

words were stilted and clipped, as though he was reading a report from the newspapers. She also sensed he wasn't too happy he'd shared the information with her and in an effort to hopefully make him feel better, she shared some more, wanting him to know she understood.

'My parents have passed away, too. Well, my biological mother abandoned us when we were almost five years old but then my father married a wonderful woman, Tish. *She* was a real mother to us.'

'How long ago did they pass away?'

'Almost two and a half years ago.' She sighed. 'And I miss them every day.'

'There's so much love in your voice when you talk about them,' Archer offered quietly. 'I envy that.'

Cora smiled sadly. 'As you've pointed out, being one of three means I'm never alone. We've always laughed together, cried together and shared our dreams together. Sharing a pain really does help those wounds to heal.' She thought back to the darkest time in her own life and how Molly and Stacey had helped her through it, had stood by her, nursed her, visited her, assisted in whatever way they could in order for her to re-gain her health.

'Hmm.' He thought on her words for a moment before continuing, keeping the focus on her and definitely away from him. She had the sense that he didn't particularly want to talk about his past, especially where it pertained to his parents. 'So…being one of three, I guess that means you're not a very selfish person. You would have always had to share everything.'

Cora shrugged. 'I don't know any other way.'

'Huh. Interesting.'

She felt Nee-Ty sag against her and she glanced down at him. 'Is he asleep?' she asked quietly.

Archer nodded, almost visibly relieved to have the conversation shifted away from the more personal topic of family. 'I hate to think how he's going to react when he sees his village. Will he fully comprehend what's happened?'

'It's not a nice feeling. Seeing the only life you've ever known disappear.' Cora brushed a hand against Nee-Ty's forehead, pushing his hair gently back from his face. 'Not that I've had my entire village destroyed,' she added quickly. 'But when my mother left, from what my five-year-old memory can recall, my father repainted the house, bought different furniture.' She shrugged. 'That sort of thing.'

'He wanted to remove any trace of her,' Archer stated. 'Of the things she'd done, like choosing furniture or painting a room.'

'I guess so.' She was also intrigued at the way his words were framed with a hint of cynicism. Had Archer experienced this, too? Had his life been destroyed? 'Anyway, years later, after he'd married Tish, he moved us all to the other side of Australia mid-year and that's when every-thing changed.'

'Did you resent him?'

'For taking us away from everything we'd ever known? A little but not for long. Stacey felt it far more deeply than I did but I think that move was the inception of my need for adventure, my need to discover new things. Until we started at a new school, living in a different house, mak-ing new friends, I hadn't realised there had been anything missing from my life.'

'You like adventure, then, do you, Dr Wilton?' He raised an eyebrow as though quite intrigued at this new piece of information.

'I do.'

Archer spread his arm out, indicating their present predicament. 'And yesterday's adventure? Was that an adrenaline high for you?'

'No.' She laughed with a hint of denial. 'Yesterday's cyclone was one adventure I wouldn't have minded missing.'

'But tell me truthfully...' Archer leaned a little closer to her, swatting at a nearby insect. 'Although it was hairy and scary and dicey and filled with urgency, when we reached that cave, when we were all finally safe, didn't you get that rush of pure elation? That thrill at having beaten nature's elements and cheated death? That victorious buzz?'

'Uh...I think, as you might care to recall, that once we were safe in the cave, I basically passed out.'

Archer leaned back and rubbed his chin with his thumb and forefinger, as though processing her words thoughtfully. 'True, true. But were you elated exhausted or terrified exhausted?'

Cora chuckled. 'I think I was just exhausted exhausted.'

She looked into his bright blue eyes, admiring the way they seemed to sparkle with life, with energy, with power. How was it possible that a man she knew so little about could entice such a warm reaction to flow through her with just a look? She didn't even know his surname and yet right at this moment she was having a difficult time to stop staring at him. Who *was* Archer? He'd been direct, brisk, surprised and thoughtful. During the past few minutes while they'd been talking he'd been hesitant, clipped, and now, she realised, he even seemed a little more relaxed in her presence.

She continued to hold his gaze for a fraction of a second longer before forcing herself to look away. Yes, he was her superhero but, from the sounds of it, coming to her rescue may have been his way of searching and receiving the adrenaline high a lot of thrill-seeking men craved. 'I'm guessing you like the whole "battling Mother Nature" sort of thing?'

'I guess I do but, rest assured, I wouldn't have ventured out into such a storm if I hadn't been specifically looking for you and Nee-Ty.' He indicated to her and the boy with a firm hand, fingers together. 'But…I confess I *did* get an adrenaline boost when we finally made it to the cave. Objective completed.'

'So you get an adrenaline high when you've completed your objective?'

Archer shrugged then checked the time on his watch. 'Perhaps I do. I've never really thought about it in such great detail before.' He stood and stretched his long legs, raising his arms above his head. 'We should get moving.'

Cora wasn't listening. Instead, she was hard pressed not to watch him, her mind registering the minutest of movements: his triceps clearly visible beneath the long-sleeved shirt he'd rolled up to his elbows; the tip of his shirt breaking loose from the waistband of his green fatigues allowing a perfect strip of male lower abdominals to be visible for a few seconds; and one raised eyebrow when she finally raised her gaze to meet his.

'Now *that's* an adrenaline rush in itself,' he murmured appreciatively, and her eyes widened in alarm. Was he teasing her? She hardly knew this man and here she was, openly ogling him. What had she been thinking! Cora knew she should probably look away, should blush, should feel embarrassed at being caught staring at him, but she didn't. Instead, she continued to look directly into his gorgeous blue eyes, eyes that were exactly the same shade as the clear sky above.

'Well…' She slowly shrugged one shoulder, angling her head to the side in what she hoped was a provocative manner. Two could play at this strange sort of stand-off they seemed to be having. 'Then I'm more than happy to provide you with your fix any time you need it.'

CHAPTER THREE

IF STACEY HAD heard her sister utter those evocative words she would have gasped with shock. Cora knew she sounded more like her other sister Molly, as that was exactly the type of thing she would have said. And now she completely understood the appeal. Saying such things to a man, especially one as gorgeous as Archer, was quite empowering.

Archer's answer was to throw back his head and laugh. Cora frowned for a moment. Perhaps she'd done something wrong, especially as he appeared to be finding her attempts at flirting quite hilarious.

'It's not *that* funny,' she remarked, frowning at him.

His grin eased from his lips and he quickly shoved his hands into his pockets. 'I wasn't laughing *at* you, Cora.' Archer looked down at the ground for a moment before meeting her gaze once more. 'It was just the absurdity of the entire situation. We're in the middle of nowhere, having come through an exceedingly stressful situation, and now, sitting beneath trees that have been uprooted, we're flirting.'

'We were flirting?' Cora was pleased with his explanation and at her words he chuckled again, the rich sound washing over her like a soothing melody. Unfortunately, it couldn't have been that soothing as Nee-Ty started to stir. She stood and brushed her trousers down, pleased to get the blood pumping back through her legs, before picking up the still drowsy little boy.

'Ready?' Archer shrugged the pack onto his back and checked his watch once more.

'How are we going for time?' she asked, shifting Nee-Ty in her arms so his little head was still resting on her shoulder.

'We're doing well.'

'And you know which way we're going?'

'Of course.' He looked at her as though she'd grown an extra head. 'I know my way around this entire island.'

'Impressive.' She wondered just how long he'd been visiting Tarparnii. 'Of course,' she said, remembering their earlier conversation. 'You used to come here with Daniel in the school holidays when you were boys.'

'That's right.' His words were back to being direct and she had the feeling that he wasn't all that interested in talking any more. She followed a few steps behind him, watching where he was putting his feet and copying his movements. She had noticed that he'd decreased the length of his stride in order to make it easier for her and she silently thanked him for his thoughtfulness.

'So that was military school?'

'Yes.'

'I didn't know Daniel had been at military school but, then, there's a lot about Daniel I don't know.' They walked on for a few minutes in silence, Cora wondering whether Archer was now regretting their earlier conversation, the one where he'd laughed and smiled, because for some reason he didn't seem too interested in doing either now.

'Have you actually been in the armed forces or did military school put you off?'

Archer looked over his shoulder at her, as

though annoyed she was still questioning him. 'I was an army medic for over ten years.'

'Huh.' She nodded. 'That makes sense now.'

'Pardon?'

'The way you were able to bound over boulders, to rescue young children and damsels in distress.' She shifted Nee-Ty in her arms, the little boy having slowly woken up from his nap. 'How you made a fire, kept us all safe last night, had a pack that seems to be more like a magician's bag as you pulled out exactly what we needed most.'

'I've been trained to do those things.'

'Well trained, I'd say. Remember, you saved my life.'

'Just…drop it.' Archer's tone was curt and Cora felt as though he'd just told her off. She was only trying to show her gratitude but apparently he didn't want it. Feeling slightly miffed, she shifted Nee-Ty on her hip as she followed him.

'I'm only saying thank you,' she muttered.

'Pardon?'

'Nothing.'

Archer shook his head as though he didn't want to be reminded of his heroic acts and yet he still stepped to the side, holding a large clump of foliage out of her way so that she and Nee-Ty could make it safely past. She ducked her head and placed a hand on Nee-Ty's head to ensure he didn't get hit by a low-hanging branch.

'I was just grateful to find the two of you together,' he stated as she navigated her way through the gap he'd made. 'With the way the wind speed was increasing, I wouldn't have had time to search for two people separately.' He followed her through and let the foliage go.

'And we both appreciate your expertise and care.' She paused for a moment and looked up at him, their gazes meeting and holding for what seemed like an eternity but in reality was just a matter of seconds. There was determination in her words. It didn't matter whether or not he wanted to hear it, *she* needed to say it. 'Thank you, Archer.'

'I believe you've already thanked me. Several times.' With that, he struck out at a faster pace than before. Perhaps he thought if he kept her huffing and puffing beside him she wouldn't have the opportunity to ask him any more questions.

Cora took the hint and for the next fifteen minutes they walked on in relative silence except for Archer saying things like, 'Duck your head,' or, 'Go slowly through here,' or, 'Would you like me to take the boy?'

Although Nee-Ty wasn't all that heavy, carrying him for such a long time was starting to put a strain on her shoulder muscles, but Cora was more concerned that the little boy had no shoes on. Granted, he probably traipsed around these parts quite often in bare feet, but after the storm they had no idea of knowing exactly what they might find on the ground.

When they came into a wider, more open area, Nee-Ty raised his head from her shoulder and wriggled in her arms. Cora instantly let him down and he ran off, obviously recognising their surroundings as the border of his village.

They both quickened their pace to keep up with him but when she saw him standing in the centre of his village, the huts either blown over or in pieces around him, Cora's heart ached with sympathy for the little boy. His world, probably the only one he'd ever known, was gone. From far away, up near the cave, the village had looked like a tiny mess, as if a child had broken and discarded their toys, but now, standing in the middle of the devastation, she shook her head.

'Grandmother? Grandmother?' he kept calling over and over. 'Where is my grandmother? The people?' His guttural Tarparnese pierced her soul and tears instantly sprang to her eyes. 'Grandmother!'

Cora held out her hands towards him as she came closer, wanting to comfort him in any way she could, but with his long stride Archer reached Nee-Ty first and bent down, speaking with compassion.

'The storm wrecked the village,' he told the boy. 'The people are safe. We will find your grandmother and the rest of your tribe.'

'No. No. Just Grandmother,' he said over and over again. 'No mother and father. Only Grandmother.'

'Oh, no.' Cora placed a hand over her mouth as she mentally translated the little boy's words. 'Did he just say he had no parents?'

Archer met her gaze, holding it for a split second. 'Yes.'

'The poor baby.' Unbidden tears sprang to her

eyes as she held out her hands to Nee-Ty. He raised his hands, more than happy to be drawn into her embrace. Cora placed her hand on Nee-Ty's back, rubbing gently. 'We will help you. We will take you to your grandmother.' Her words were soft and as the little boy started to cry she held him tighter, wanting to do everything she could to reassure him.

Archer stepped away from them, as though uncomfortable by the scene, unsure what to do. She was vaguely aware of him picking up bits of rubble, sorting through it to see if there was anything worth salvaging.

When Archer's radio crackled to life, indicating they were back in range of the frequency, he quickly answered the call, talking briskly to whomever was on the other end.

'We're back in the village, not far from the road,' he responded when told that a transport was nearing their position to pick them up. 'OK. Confirm pick-up in twenty minutes.' He once more reassured the person on the other end of the radio that they were all fine and after he signed off he turned to face Cora.

Nee-Ty had stopped crying. Cora was wiping

away his tears with her fingers but both of them were staring at him. He spread his arms wide, indicating the area around them. 'We have fifteen minutes to see if there's anything worth salvaging to return to the villagers before we need to leave for the rendezvous site.'

'Sounds like a good idea.' She explained to Nee-Ty what was happening, telling him they wanted to find precious things to take back to his tribe, and after sniffing and brushing some tears from his eyes he nodded and wriggled from her arms. He ran over to one specific pile of rubble and pointed eagerly. Archer willingly obliged and lifted the large branches and bits of the thatched roof from the area. When there was enough room, Nee-Ty crawled in there, ignoring to Cora's concerned protests. But a moment later he appeared again, holding a wooden mask, which was about the size of Archer's hand. The mask had been lovingly carved and painted, and when he could finally stand up Nee-Ty held the mask up to his face. 'Mask.'

Archer crouched down to look at the beautifully made article. 'Is this your mask?' he asked the boy in Tarparnese, and Nee-Ty nodded eagerly. 'Did your father make this?'

Nee-Ty nodded again as he lowered the mask, his face beaming with a wide smile.

'He probably carved it while his *par'machkai*, his life mate, was pregnant with Nee-Ty and decorated it on his birth.'

'Is that one of the Tarparnese rituals? I haven't come across it.' Cora knelt down and held out her hand to the mask. 'May I look?' she asked, but Nee-Ty didn't hand it to her. Instead, he held it out for her to see but didn't want to let it go.

'A lot of villages are embracing new ways of doing things,' Archer stated as he stood and started looking through another pile of debris. 'They call it "white man's way" because their elders can see the benefits for such changes, but a lot of inland villages, such as this one, situated further away from the main roads and well-populated areas, still hold firm to the traditions of the past. The mask he has represents the dreams and the direction Nee-Ty's father would have planned for him throughout his life.'

'What do all the markings mean?' Cora stared

at the mask as she asked the question, impressed by the intricate artwork.

'I'm not one hundred per cent sure but Daniel will be able to interpret the markings and the symbols so that Nee-Ty, with this mask, will be able to walk forward with confidence towards his future. When he becomes a man, at the ripe old age of fourteen, he is supposed to accept the mask in a ceremony where he vows to pursue the direction outlined by his father.'

As though Nee-Ty could understand every word Archer was saying, he beamed with purpose. His smile spoke volumes. He had his mask. He was happy.

She looked across at Archer to find him regarding Nee-Ty closely. 'He's a resilient little chap, isn't he.' It wasn't a question but more of a statement and Cora nodded in agreement. 'That type of quality will stand him in good stead throughout his life.' He met her gaze and she could hear the determination in his voice as he spoke.

'Let's reunite this brave little boy with his grandmother so he can be even happier. I think he's earned it.'

* * *

They continued to find a few more bits and pieces that they thought might be precious to the villagers who had once lived here, then headed to the road.

'The transport should be here...' Archer looked towards the curved, narrow road, which bore an uncanny resemblance to a long pit of mud. There was no sign of the truck so he checked his watch. 'Any moment now.' He checked the road again and Cora couldn't help but smile at Archer's wry grin. Rarely, in the jungles of Tarparnii, did anything run on time, especially not transportation.

Archer angled his head, listening closely as though trying to hear the truck's engine. 'Aha!' He looked up the road again and, sure enough, the huge front section of the old army transport truck was just visible around the corner of the road, trees and foliage still blocking the rest of the vehicle from view. 'Here it is.'

'Your psychic abilities are amazing,' she teased, stepping back a little as the heavy-duty tyres on the truck flicked bits of mud up into the air. As the truck drew closer, slowing down for them, Nee-Ty, who was safe in her arms, holding tight to his mask, seemed to lean into her more.

'It's all right,' she told him. 'We're taking you to your grandmother. We need to go in the...' She stared at Archer. 'What's the word for truck?'

'T'kenom.'

Nee-Ty shook his head before burying it in Cora's shoulder. 'Have you ever been on a truck?' she asked the boy. Nee-Ty's answer was to whimper and clutch his mask tighter to him.

'Cora will stay with you.' Archer tried to help but when Nee-Ty continued to whimper, he met her gaze. He seemed to be slightly bewildered by the child and his tone held a tinge of impatience. 'He can't stay here. He must get on the truck,' he said in English, as though he wasn't quite sure how to deal with the situation. Cyclones? Yes. Navigating the land? Yes. A scared three-year-old? No.

'It's OK.' Cora gave him a pointed look. 'Just relax. I know you're all schedules and keeping things running on time but Nee-Ty's scared. This is a big deal for him.'

Archer stood his ground and put his hands on his hips. 'Other people are relying on the supplies in that truck. This whole situation…' he indicated the truck, which had finally come to a stop '…is bigger than Nee-Ty's fear.'

'I understand.' Cora tried not to grit her teeth. 'Can't you just put that military side of yours away for a few minutes so I can reassure him? To take him kicking and screaming onto the transport isn't going to be good for anyone.'

'If he's that scared, there's always—'

'Don't you dare think of sedating him.' She shifted Nee-Ty in her arms. 'Just load the things we've been able to salvage into the truck while I talk quietly to Nee-Ty.'

He looked a little sceptical but she simply turned her back on him and carried Nee-Ty over to an uprooted tree stump, where she sat down, talking quietly to the boy, reassuring him as best she could.

'Cora?' Archer called a few minutes later, tapping his watch. 'We really need to get going.'

'Understood,' she replied, her tone still laced with annoyance at him, before returning her attention to Nee-Ty. 'I know you're frightened,' she reassured him, hoping she had the right words and wasn't getting her Tarparnese all mixed up. 'But you are a brave boy and you have your mask.'

Nee-Ty eased back, looking at the mask gripped between his fingers, then at Cora. She nodded and smiled. 'We can find your grandmother. What do you say?' She waited for Nee-Ty's approval. After a moment he nodded but still clung to her for dear life.

'Well done,' a deep voice said from just to her left. She turned, surprised to see Archer there as she started walking back towards the truck, Nee-Ty burying his face in her shoulder once more. 'You're clearly quite adept at talking to children.'

'I have siblings, remember.' Her words were still clipped and Archer nodded as though he realised she was still annoyed at him. He placed his hands at her waist in order to help her into the truck, especially as she still needed to hold on to Nee-Ty. Cora tried not to react to the way his warm hands caused a riot of sensations to instantly spread throughout her entire body.

'Talking to children is one thing I've never really felt comfortable with.' His words were spoken close to her ear, as though he didn't want anyone else to hear.

'Is that your way of apologising for your behaviour?' Cora turned her head to look at him but immediately realised her mistake because all she was aware of was just how close their faces were to each other. Her gaze dipped momentarily to his mouth before she met his eyes once more.

'Uh…' Her mind went completely blank, and if anyone had asked her name, she wouldn't have been able to tell them. It felt like minutes, rather than seconds, had ticked by, just the two of them, caught in a bubble of time, staring at each other. Someone called Archer's name and he immediately turned his head, effectively breaking the moment.

Cora stumbled into the rear tray of the truck and sat down, unsure whether her legs would continue to support her given her entire body was suffused with heat and an overwhelming awareness of just how big and tender Archer could be. She recalled the way he'd laughed when they'd stopped for their rest, the memory bringing a small smile to her lips as she watched him climb into the rear of the truck. He glanced her way.

'You two OK?'

Cora opened her mouth to speak but no sound came out, so she closed her mouth and nodded instead. Unable to hold his gaze any longer, she dipped her head and whispered in Nee-Ty's ear, soothing the little boy with her words, especially when the truck's engine roared to life. A moment later they were off, bumping along the uneven road.

There were several other people, some native Tarparniians and some PMA workers. There were also several crates of PMA medical equipment stacked and secured at the opposite end to the entrance. The majority of people sat on the tray of the truck, a few stood, hanging on to the metal frame, which was covered with a heavy tarpaulin.

Archer was greeted by a few people also travelling in the truck. He introduced Cora and Nee-Ty before listening to other stories of how people had found shelter from the cyclone and the havoc it had wreaked. Most of the people on the transport were on their way to a large village where a clinic was being set up to deal with the large number of injured people.

'Cora,' Archer said after a while, and she looked up at him as he held on to the metal frame. She tried not to focus on his stance, the way his biceps flexed, the way his long legs supported him. Instead, she forced herself to listen intently to whatever he was about to say. She was a professional and professionals didn't ogle their colleagues. 'It didn't even occur to me to ask earlier, but where are you stationed?'

'Mainly in Jalak's village.'

'I know it well.' He nodded. Cora couldn't believe how odd it felt to be having a normal conversation after everything they'd been through. 'I'm generally stationed in Nahkala Tarvon's village. She's Daniel's mother,' he added. 'Have you met her?'

'I haven't but I'm happy to go wherever I'm needed,' she stated, directing her comments not only to Archer but to Sue and Keith, the new PMA workers she'd just met. Both of them were in organising mode, talking on satellite phones or two-way radios, jotting down notes and other bits of pertinent information.

'You're not too tired?' Sue asked as Keith's satellite phone rang again.

'I'll live,' Cora replied.

'Good. Because we would love an extra set of hands once we get to Nahkala's village.'

'Of course.' Cora had no idea where she was going to find the extra energy but she always did. It was part of her medical training: to find those inner reserves when it mattered the most and right now, there were people who needed their help.

'Excellent.' Sue wrote Cora's name on a piece of paper. 'And I take it I can add you to my list, Archer?'

'Of course,' he replied as the truck went over a large bump. Everyone in the back was jostled and Cora nearly fell forward, almost landing on Nee-Ty, but Archer's big strong arms instantly came about her, keeping her as upright as possible.

'Are you all right?' He'd crouched down, his words close to her ear, his breath fanning her neck, and Cora instantly closed her eyes, trying to ignore the sensation. The only reason she was responding like this to the man she'd called her own personal superhero was simply because of their shared ordeal. She didn't know him and that was a fact she had to keep remembering.

'Y-yes.' She cleared her throat and glanced at him. 'Thanks. And you?'

He eased back, putting some much-needed distance between them. 'I'm perfectly fine. Thank you.' He turned his attention to the boy, who was still clinging tightly to his mask but wasn't burying himself inside Cora's arms as much as he had before. 'Do you like the truck ride?' he asked Nee-Ty in the native language, and the child nodded. 'Excellent.'

'Did you want to sit down?' Cora asked, looking around her. 'I'm sure I could shift over a bit more.'

'I'll be fine standing.' Yet he didn't make any effort to stand but instead remained crouched down near her, balancing with great difficulty as the transport continued to rumble its way along the very uneven ground.

'Cora, what's your last name?' Sue asked, interrupting them.

'Wilton,' she supplied.

Sue chuckled. 'Wild and Wilton.' She wrote their names down. 'Sounds like a law firm.'

'I think it sounds like a pop band from the nineteen-eighties,' Keith added as he finished his call.

'Huh?' Cora glanced at Archer. 'Wild and Wilton?'

'Wild. That's my surname,' Archer offered.

'Archer Wild?' She grinned because, from what she'd seen, Archer was anything but wild. Sure, he was outdoorsy and great to have around in a crisis, but wild? That wouldn't have been one of the adjectives she would have used to describe him. 'That's your name?'

'It is.'

'Oh, sorry.' Sue looked puzzled. 'I thought you two had already met.'

'We have,' Cora replied. 'He saved my life.'

'She passed out from exhaustion and mild hypothermia,' Archer stated, as though he didn't want any of the credit for the gallant and heroic things he'd done. 'We didn't really have the opportunity to exchange pleasantries.'

'You knew my name,' she countered.

'You are correct. It was completely remiss

of me not to have introduced myself properly. Please allow me to remedy the oversight immediately.' He held out his hand to her and she placed her free hand in it, the other still holding Nee-Ty close.

'I'm Dr Archer Franklin Brace Wild. It's a pleasure to make your acquaintance.' He shook her hand. Cora ignored the tingles she felt shoot up her arm. The way he was making her feel was simply because of the past twelve or so hours. Nothing more.

'That's quite a mouthful of a name you have there.'

He shrugged on shoulder. 'It's just a name.' He was about to say more when the truck jostled again and this time Cora was thrown off to the side, Nee-Ty slipping from her arms and Archer's heavy frame landing on top of her.

For one split second they were almost nose to nose as he quickly raised himself up on his arms so he didn't squash her. They stared at each other, their breaths mingling, their hearts pounding. Blood pumped faster throughout Cora's body, every sense, every nerve and fibre of her being one hundred per cent aware of this amazing man. Not only had he saved her life but he'd awakened senses that had lain dormant for a very long time, senses she'd done her best to quash and forget. Now they were zinging with excited anticipation because of his extremely close proximity.

'Archer Wild.' His name was a whispered caress on her lips as she stared into his perfectly blue eyes. 'I like it.'

CHAPTER FOUR

CORA COULDN'T BELIEVE just how intense she felt having Archer's body so close to hers. Within a second he'd raised himself up onto his hands to ensure she wasn't crushed by his weight.

'Are you all right?' His words were soft, deep and filled with concern. Couldn't he feel it? The tension that seemed to buzz between them? This wasn't the first time it had happened during their short acquaintance. What it might mean she had no clue.

'Uh-huh.' She'd tried to speak a normal word, to form a sentence to let him know that she hadn't been hurt, and yet her brain didn't seem able to compute anything other than just how close he was to her right at this point in time.

He pursed his lips and nodded, levering himself back into a seated position before helping her to sit up. 'Good. Good.' He looked around for Nee-Ty, checking the boy to ensure he was all right. Physically the child was fine but the mask had skittered from his little fingers and he was now frantically trying to find it.

'I'll get it,' Archer assured him, spotting the mask between two of the medical crates. 'Sit with Cora.' Nee-Ty did as he was told while Archer retrieved the mask and handed it back to the eager three-year-old.

He checked on some of the other people around them, pleased no one had been hurt. He tried not to focus on Cora, on ensuring she was in a more stable position so that if the truck jostled again she wouldn't get hurt. He had to remind himself that now that she'd been found, now that they were safe on the truck, Cora Wilton was no longer his responsibility. She was a fully grown woman…one who had felt incredible in his arms, especially last night as she'd slept, snuggling close in order to keep warm.

When he'd first found her he'd been relieved she'd managed to connect with the boy, that he hadn't had to go looking for two separate people. Then, when she'd looked up at him, pushing the hair from her face, her brown eyes wide with fear, his heart had constricted. That had only ever happened to him once before in his life and the woman who had caused him to experience such a sensation had eventually become his wife.

That was why Archer needed to keep busy; needed to make sure his thoughts remained on task. They were headed into a situation where a lot of people had been hurt, where a lot of people required his expertise. In times like these he was a general surgeon first. Everything else came second. He knew many of the medical staff who came to Tarparnii to work with PMA were experienced in a variety of different fields but stretched their skills into other disciplines. He glanced over at Cora, who was once again sitting cross-legged on the tray of the tuck, holding Nee-Ty close in her arms, looking anywhere but at him—or so it seemed.

The little boy was clearly taken with her and Archer could understand why. He didn't know much about Cora Wilton, other than her name and that she'd risked her life to rescue a three-year-old boy. He had no idea what type of doctor she was, or where she lived in Australia.

He knew she was a triplet and that she was

very close to her family. The love he'd heard in her voice when she'd spoken to her sibling, the relief he'd seen on her face at being able to re-assure those who loved her that she was indeed all right, was evidence of this. What he didn't know was how Cora would perform in an emer-gency medical situation or how she might feel about taking orders from him.

It wasn't that he was dictatorial, he respected all his colleagues, but sometimes, in height-ened medical situations, he knew he could come across as being rather brisk, even if that wasn't his intention. He blamed his loveless upbring-ing and the military for that trait.

She'd called him her superhero and he'd cringed at such a label. Labels weren't good. He knew that of old as his father had labelled him as useless, ridiculous and a complete disap-pointment. It was no good for anyone to think of him as anything other than a man who'd been trained with specific skills. It was why he'd ac-tually asked Cora to stop—otherwise she would end up being sadly disillusioned when she dis-covered that he was nothing special.

Only Georgie, his childhood friend and the

woman who had come to mean so much to him, had seen the good in him—had encouraged him to strive for what he wanted. He closed his eyes, pushing the image of Georgie's face from his mind. Now was not the time to think about his wife.

He opened his eyes, determined to deal with his present situation: that of contemplating the different scenarios they might encounter when the truck reached its destination at Nahkala Tarvon's village. But his gaze seemed to instantly seek out Cora. She was chatting with Sue while reassuring Nee-Ty by stroking the little boy's back. Sue laughed at something Cora had said and Archer watched as a lovely smile lit Cora's face. Her hair might be all tousled, her clothes might be dirty, her arms might be tired, but when she smiled like that it was as though a rainbow had appeared after a fierce storm.

Archer raised his hands overhead and gripped the metal bar, using it to steady himself as he forced himself to look away. Why was it he was having so much difficulty in controlling his thoughts? Why couldn't he just switch off the image of Cora's beguiling smile? Of how it had felt to hold her in his arms? Of fixating on just how close his mouth had been to her purely kissable lips?

When the truck started to slow, the road becoming more winding as they headed towards Nahkala's village, Archer felt his professional self finally kick into gear. From what Sue and Keith had told him, there was another team of PMA staff who should already have reached the destination to begin setting up the makeshift medical clinic that would help deal with the increase of patients they would see.

Nahkala's village had permanent clinic buildings and operating theatres but for the next few days they would definitely need those extra tents for the plethora of people they'd be seeing from the after-effects of the cyclone. This time there would be additional tents for triage, general consulting, treatment of wounds such as basic cuts and abrasions, as well as a plaster tent for broken bones and a few for patients and families to shelter beneath while they waited.

The phone in his pocket started ringing and he quickly retrieved it, pleased to hear Daniel's voice on the other end. 'We should be there soon.

What's the situation?' he asked, listening to what his friend was saying.

'What sort of doctor are you?' he heard Sue ask Cora. Archer listened to the answer, knowing it would give him a better idea of how best to make use of her skills once they arrived. She was a colleague and, as such, he needed to ensure he treated her in a friendly and professional manner, just as he did the rest of his colleagues. Any connection that might have formed due to their intense contact over the past twelve or so hours would begin to dissipate once they reintegrated themselves with the other PMA staff.

'GP with a diploma in emergency medicine,' Cora replied. 'After my first stint with PMA I realised I needed to enhance my qualifications when I returned to Australia, and I have to say it really has made a difference this time around.'

Sue nodded. 'I did the same thing after my first stint. Returned home and did more training. I also think your second term with PMA runs more smoothly.'

'Because you know what to expect,' Cora finished with a smile. 'Agreed. How long have you been volunteering with PMA, Sue?' she asked, glancing at Archer as he finished his phone call.

'Ooh, too many years to count.' Sue chuckled. 'Almost as many as Keith, but nowhere near as many as Archer.

'Oh?' Cora raised an eyebrow at Archer. 'And just how long have you been working with PMA?'

'I volunteered all through medical school and when I left the army four years ago I became a permanent member of the Tarparnii team.'

Keith nodded. 'Archer's been here so long that working in a normal hospital with up-to-date equipment and technology is a foreign world to him.'

Cora smiled, watching how Archer seemed to easily accept the good-natured teasing of his friends. It was interesting to observe the way he interacted with his other colleagues. He was personable enough but also appeared to have a shield up, a barrier that she doubted many would break through. Was that another side-effect of all those boarding schools? Of his time in the military? Keeping an emotional distance? She shook her head, knowing there was no way she'd ever be able to live in such a world.

She liked getting to know people, figuring out what made them tick and how they could enhance her life. She also liked being alone, taking a nature walk, climbing rocks, abseiling. Those times when she was by herself helped her to reflect inwards, to get in touch with who she was at the core of Cora. Then afterwards she would spend time with her friends, her family and absorb all the happiness and love, recharging her internal batteries.

The squealing brakes of the truck snapped her thoughts back to the present, Nee-Ty tensing up with fear at the sound. Cora instantly soothed him as the truck finally came to a stop. Archer called for everyone's attention before they started to move.

'OK, listen up. First priority is unloading the truck. Second is to report to Daniel and sign in. Remember, it's important to sign in because we need to know everyone's whereabouts. I also think it goes without saying that there's no going off on your own anywhere.' He paused after giving the instructions in English then eased into guttural Tarparnese, repeating the instructions. Even the non-PMA people on the truck needed to register their presence in the village. During heightened circumstances, such yesterday's cyclone, a certain level of control was required.

He continued to give a rundown of the situation, assigning jobs where necessary. Cora's job was to head to the triage tent once it was set up. Archer's words were controlled, brisk and professional. The military man she'd first encountered was back.

'OK. Initial job is to get this truck unloaded.' He nodded once as he glanced at the people around him. 'Let's get to work.'

'Cora, can you take a look at this patient? She's been complaining of abdominal pain, saying it's been there for almost half a day.' Stella, a young nurse from Canada, had been working alongside Cora in the triage tent for the past four hours. At times, just when they thought they had the amount of patients under control, a truck would arrive, bringing more injured and sick people who required their attention.

Cora reached for a new set of gloves and

headed over to where Stella had just finished assessing their latest patient. 'Hello. I'm Dr Cora,' she said to her patient in Tarparnese. 'Can you describe the pain for me?'

As she listened to the pain the woman described Cora frowned, thinking quickly. She hooked her stethoscope into her ears and listened carefully to the sounds of the woman's abdomen. She asked her other questions, such as whether she'd been tired, vomiting, having diarrhoea or a temperature. The woman said she hadn't, just the abdominal pain, and it had only started about half a day ago, just before the cyclone.

Cora checked the chart for the information Stella had already gathered before deciding to gently palpate the abdomen. When she did, she found increased tenderness on the left side, rather than the right.

'Not appendicitis?' Stella asked.

Cora shook her head before asking her patient, 'Have you swallowed anything unusual?'

At the question, Cora saw her patient look a little sheepish but the next moment had another attack of pain, almost doubling over.

'I'd like to get Archer to take a look at her

but chances are she's swallowed something she shouldn't have and her intestines aren't too happy about it.'

'Oh, for an X-ray machine,' Stella remarked, before writing a note for one of the runners. A lot of the older teenagers from Nahkala's village had volunteered to deliver messages from tent to tent, saving the medical staff the bother of having to find the consultants they required without diminishing the care of their patients.

It was only a few minutes later that Archer came into the tent, the note from the runner in his hand. 'You wanted me?' he stated, looking directly into Cora's brown eyes. The two of them had been apart for about the past five hours and yet for some strange reason it had felt much longer. He'd concentrated on his work, giving his patients the best attention and care, and yet until he'd walked in here and seen her he hadn't realised how tense he'd become.

'Uh...' Cora stared blankly at him for a moment, all rational and reasonable thought eluding her. How did he know she wanted him? What had Stella written on that note? She blinked once, twice before he clarified.

'You have a patient for me to assess?'

'Er...yes.' At the mention of their patient the world around them seemed to return and Cora instantly held out her stethoscope to him. 'Have a listen to her abdomen—pain localised to the left side, no nausea, vomiting, diarrhoea. No headaches, elevated temperature or loss of consciousness.'

'And when did the pains begin to occur?' He hooked the stethoscope into his ears and listened to the patient's abdomen, as Cora had instructed.

'Less than twenty-four hours' duration.'

Archer spoke softly to the patient, asking her questions to confirm what Cora had already told him in English. Once his examination was complete he turned to Cora, his tone professional. 'Suspicions?'

'Without photographic evidence for confirmation, I'd suggest the patient has swallowed a foreign object of some kind.'

'And I'll add to that by deducing the object is small and was probably swallowed just before they were evacuated.'

Cora's eyes widened. 'Why couldn't they just carry—?'

'It was as important to her as Nee-Ty's mask is to him. It's not the first time I've seen this happen. Swallow a small object, wait for it to pass through your system and then retrieve it.'

She shook her head from side to side. 'Well, something's gone wrong with that plan. Any guesses as to what it might be?'

Archer turned back to their patient and asked her some more questions, telling her it was all right to admit that she'd swallowed something, they just needed to know what it was, but she refused to tell them.

'Without X-ray facilities it's going to be easiest to open her up and retrieve whatever it is before it causes more damage.' Archer found the patient's chart and wrote on it. 'I'll go prep a theatre.' He turned and took a few steps away before he stopped. 'Would you like to scrub in and assist?' he asked over his shoulder.

'Uh…yeah.' A smile tugged at her lips. 'I'd love that.'

'OK. I'll arrange for you to be relieved here.'

And within the hour Cora found herself standing across the operating table from Archer, assisting with the removal of a beautiful diamond and emerald ring from their patient's small intestine.

'No wonder she's been in pain.' Archer dropped the ring into a nearby kidney dish. 'I'll just have a little look around, make sure there are no other problems and then close. Would you mind retracting, please?'

He was clever, thorough and respectful, and not only to his patients. It was true that the theatre surroundings were incredibly bare, with only Archer, one nurse, the anaesthetist and herself to perform the surgery. Even then, the nurse had to leave halfway through but Cora was more than able to do what was needed.

There were no X-ray machines, or small cameras used to perform a colonoscopy or endoscopy, nor any of the other expensive equipment usually housed in the theatre blocks in big teaching hospitals. Yet Archer really did seem to be quite at home in these surroundings.

'You clearly love what you do,' she told him as they degowned.

'I do. I like helping people as I am sure, do you.'

'That's why I'm here.' She smiled up at him

as the anaesthetist took their patient to the recovery tent, leaving them alone.

He picked up the case notes and leaned against the wall, writing up his operation report. 'At least the red tape here isn't as meticulous as in a hospital.'

'And I would have thought, with you being Mr Military, that you'd be a natural at navigating red tape.'

'That's Dr Military to you,' he remarked, glancing up at her, a slight twinkle in his eyes. Cora instantly smiled at him. It was the man she'd chatted with yesterday, the one who had laughed with abandon. His smile increased and he returned his attention to the case notes. A moment later he signed his name and closed them. 'So...Cora, would you like to see if we can find a cup of something delicious to drink? The women in Nahkala's village make the most perfect fruit punch thing—non-alcoholic, of course. No alcohol is permitted in this village.'

Cora was pleasantly surprised at the invitation but when she went to answer she found herself smothering an impromptu yawn. 'Oh, I'm sorry.'

'No. You're clearly tired.'

'I didn't mean to yawn like that,' she countered. 'I appreciate your invitation. Really I do.' He chuckled and she liked the sound of it. It relaxed her even more.

'It's fine, Cora. I think I know you enough to realise you wouldn't be that blatantly rude.'

'Good.' Another yawn spread through her and Archer shook his head.

'I think that's a sign that you need to find your bed, Dr Wilton. Let's go and see where we're sleeping tonight.' He indicated the case notes in his hand. 'I'll just drop these off at Recovery.'

She waited for him, both of them noticing the bright twinkling stars in the sky. 'Night-time already. This has got to be one of the longest days I've had for a very long time.' She looked up at him. 'You're probably more exhausted than I am. I haven't been doing surgery all day and I'm pretty sure I got more sleep than you last night.'

He shrugged as though he wasn't bothered by fatigue at all. 'I'll live.' They walked side by side, not wanting to rush, as though both were more than happy to prolong their conversation. 'And at least you didn't snore.' There it was again. This teasing side to him. She liked it.

'Thank goodness.'

'Nee-Ty, however, was like a chainsaw at one stage.'

She chuckled then sighed, smothering another yawn. 'Good heavens, I can't seem to stop.'

Archer looked into her beautiful face. 'It doesn't matter. Everyone's tired.' When she looked up at him, he felt as though the world had stopped spinning. The drowsiness in her eyes, the way her hair was tucked behind her ears, the soft smile on her lips—it was exactly as she'd looked last night when he'd finished stoking the fire and had checked to see if she was still cold.

Upon finding her still shivering, he'd lain next to her and the boy, drawing her closer to his body, using their natural heat to warm her up. Survival. That's what it had been and yet, for some strange reason, he was hard pressed to remove the image and sensation of her resting peacefully in his arms, as though she really didn't have a care in the world, as though she really did trust him to protect her and keep her safe.

Would she still feel that way if she slept in his arms again tonight? Archer looked away. Even the thought of wanting to spend another night with Cora Wilton in his arms should be enough to set off warning bells and alarms. She was getting too close, too fast. The fact that he'd shared information about his past, about his school with her was evidence of that. Of course, he hadn't told her half of it but, still, it wasn't like him to just open up to a woman so easily and, therefore, he would do well to put a bit of distance between them.

When they arrived at the tent set up for administration, it was to find Melora and Daniel's daughter, Simone, sitting at a table with a sheaf of papers before her. 'Hello, Cora, Archer. Ready to find out where you're sleeping tonight?'

'Yes, please.' The exhaustion in Cora's voice could not be disguised and Simone grinned. 'Everyone is like that,' the teenager told her. 'So tired and exhausted and that's the way it should be. Everybody's worked so hard today.' As Simone spoke, she looked at the papers before her and found Cora's name.

'You're in…the purple tent. It has a coloured flag out the front. It was the best way we could think of to identify each hut once it had passed the safety inspection. My younger brothers had a great time putting the flags up, too.' She grinned widely, showing her braces.

'It's great you can all help out.' Cora smiled at the teenager but couldn't help being completely conscious of the close confines of the tent and Archer's warm body so very close to her own. Her tiredness was starting to decrease her inhibitions and the sooner she managed to get some sleep, to renew her mental clarity, the better.

'Archer,' Simone consulted her lists. 'You're in the orange hut.'

'Orange, eh?' Did she detect a hint of disappointment in his tone? Cora watched him closely but could see no sign of the emotion on his face. All she saw was a man as tired as she was, eager to get some shut-eye. 'Thanks, Simone.' Archer nodded once, then turned and held the tent flap open so Cora could precede him. She thanked Simone and followed Archer out, wanting to find the purple cabin flag as soon as possible so she could crash. 'I guess, after yesterday's events, it's best if everyone is accounted for at all times, even when it comes to the sleeping arrangements.' He looked around at the different huts, looking for the ones with the purple and orange flags out the front. He hoped they were at least next to each other.

'Absolutely.' She nodded. Cora, too, had been disappointed at not being close to Archer but in hindsight perhaps that was a good thing. The man had been by her side since yesterday afternoon and, apart from treating their patients, where his attention had been solely directed towards the task at hand, Cora had become used to having him around.

She still found it difficult to believe she hadn't known him for at least a few weeks, rather than only just over twenty-four hours. How ridiculous was that! Especially given she was finding it increasingly difficult not to be very aware of him whenever he was close by. When she'd stood opposite him in Theatre, impressed by his clever hands as he'd saved someone's life, she'd had a difficult time controlling her admiration and increasing attraction to the man. He'd had to ask her twice for the retractor and she'd been embarrassed by her lack of control over her thoughts.

She needed to focus on something else, but

before she could say anything Archer asked if she knew where Nee-Ty was.

'I think he's still with his grandmother. I wouldn't mind finding him before I get settled in for the night.' She shrugged one shoulder. 'I just need to see that he's OK.'

'Understandable.' Archer pointed to the hut where they'd delivered Nee-Ty to a waiting teenager, who Nee-Ty had run to with open arms. The little boy had talked animatedly of his 'adventures' and proudly showed off the mask he'd managed to save from the wreckage of the village.

Once they'd both been satisfied that Nee-Ty would be all right, they'd headed off to the makeshift clinic and done what they did best. Now, though, after such a long day, fatigue was definitely starting to set in but Cora knew she wouldn't be able to sleep for long without reassuring herself that Nee-Ty, the little boy who had already worked his way so firmly into her heart, was indeed all right.

'He's been through a lot of trauma for a little fellow,' Archer remarked.

'I was just thinking the same thing but how much of it does he really understand?'

'Well, at least he has his grandmother to help him feel more settled. Even though they're not in their own village, at least they're together now.'

'Exactly. I wish I'd been able to see their reunion.' Cora smiled and sighed. 'The elderly grandmother, hugging her grandson. The smile on Nee-Ty's face would have been big and bright and he would have been showing her that he'd found his mask.' She sighed again, happiness filling her. 'Such a gorgeous little boy.'

'You're a very nurturing person, Cora,' he stated after a moment.

She angled her head and gave him a quizzical look. 'It's one of the reasons why I decided to pursue a career in medicine. I like caring for people, seeing them get better.'

'What are the other reasons?'

'Well, let's see. My father was a doctor and I knew Stacey was interested in following in his footsteps, which actually put me off studying medicine for a while.'

'Because you didn't want to do what your sister did?'

'Something like that. I guess, being a triplet, although you never feel alone, sometimes people don't tend to see you as individuals. Stacey, Molly and I aren't the same person but, as it turns out, all three of us ended up studying medicine.'

'What helped you decide?'

'I uh…' She paused and looked down at the ground for a moment before glancing at him once more. 'I was in a bad accident just before we turned eighteen. Fractured pelvis.'

'Among other injuries,' he stated, a hint of sympathy in his tone.

'Yes. You can't fracture your pelvis without sustaining other internal damage. I spent a lot of time in and out of hospital, having several operations, and, I don't know, while I was there I started to see the good, the skills, the hope that the nursing and medical staff shared with their patients.'

'And thus a vocation was born.'

Cora chuckled at his words, delighted he wasn't being all brisk and military while she was opening up to him. 'How about you? Why did you choose to become a doctor?'

The smile instantly slid from Archer's face and the shutters came down. 'To garner my father's approval.' His words were stilted, emotionless. Then he pointed to the large hut, where a lot of non-villagers were spending the night. 'Here we are.'

But no sooner had they entered the tent than Sue ran up to them, her face filled with distress and concern.

'I was just coming to find you both.'

'What's wrong?'

'Is it Nee-Ty?' Cora was instantly on edge.

'No. He's fine. He's with Melora's sons, sleeping in the green hut. No.' Sue shook her head. 'It's his grandmother.'

'Oh?'

'She's just passed away.'

'What?' Cora stared open-mouthed at Sue. 'But—'

'She was apparently very ill. Nahkala and the other elders have been with her for the past few hours, making arrangements, including who is to have custody of Nee-Ty.' Sue was talking fast, trying to get the information out, her eyes as wide as saucers. 'He has no other relatives,' the nurse stated. 'And the grandmother said she wanted the two of you to be his guardians.'

'Us?' Cora stared at Archer.

'No!'

CHAPTER FIVE

CORA HAD SEEN death many times throughout her life, both from a personal and professional viewpoint. She'd been in Tarparnii when patients had died and she'd been on the fringe of their rituals regarding their dead but never had she been a part of it. Why had Nee-Ty's grandmother, the matriarch of his family and his only surviving relative, handed the young boy into the care of Archer and her? Apart from seeing the grandmother when she'd been evacuated from the village, Cora had never even met the woman.

Cora and Archer had both gone to the grandmother's side, Archer talking rapidly in Tarparnese to Nahkala, who had once again explained the situation just as Sue had. It was decided not to wake Nee-Ty but to let him have a good night's sleep before the news was broken to him in the morning.

Cora's thoughts turned to the little boy and

her heart broke. He'd been so excited to be re-united with his grandmother and now he was once again all alone, just as he'd been when she'd found him on the rocks near the cave. Were the grandmother's wishes binding? Surely it was best for Nee-Ty to remain within a village settlement of his own people? She would be returning to Australia in two weeks' time, her contract up with PMA. It would be Christmas and she would be thrust into the world of crazy silliness her family enjoyed around that time of year.

And what of Archer? She wasn't even sure where he lived, especially when she'd learned he was a permanent member of the Tarparnii medical team. Did he live here? In Nahkala's village? She knew so little about him so how could she possibly entertain the thought of becoming a co-guardian of an orphaned little boy?

Cora sat outside the visitors' hut, staring into nothingness, her thoughts going from being completely jumbled to her heart breaking for the little boy who had been placed in an unsteady and precarious position, with others tasked to make the decisions that would govern his life. She couldn't help but love Nee-Ty, but was accepting guardianship of him the right thing to do?

She was already joint guardian of her younger siblings but they weren't little any more, Lydia having just turned eight. Nee-Ty was only three years old. 'The poor baby.'

'Thinking about Nee-Ty?'

Cora looked up to see her friend Melora standing next to her with a cup in her hand. 'Yes.'

'Here.' She handed Cora the cup. 'It's sweet tea. Archer asked me to bring it to you.'

'Thanks.'

'He told us what happened. I think the grandmother probably knew something wasn't right because she sent Nee-Ty to sleep in the same hut as our boys.'

'She wanted to protect him.' Cora sipped the hot tea, grateful for Archer's thoughtfulness. 'Do you know where Archer is? Last I saw him he was talking with Nahkala and some of the other village elders.'

Melora nodded. 'They're in Nahkala's hut. Daniel's there, too. They're discussing possible solutions because usually, when one head of a family passes the care of children over to another family, it's as binding as adoption. It's permanent and to break the covenant is considered a dishonour.'

'But Archer and I aren't even a couple!' Cora waved her free hand in the air and shook her head. 'I live in Australia. I don't even know where Archer lives. Yesterday morning I didn't even know he existed. How? How can I be bonded in parenthood with him for the rest of Nee-Ty's life? And what sort of life is that going to be for Nee-Ty? Is he to be raised in different countries? Australia and Tarparnii? Surely that's not going to be good for him.'

'Shh.' Melora took the cup from Cora's hands and placed it on the ground before rubbing a soothing hand on Cora's back, just as one of her sisters would. Cora closed her eyes, forcing herself to take a few deep breaths. 'We'll figure it out. Archer has the same questions but, from what he's told us, the reason the grandmother passed Nee-Ty into your care was because when he arrived in the village he couldn't stop talking about the two of you, telling her everything you'd been through while you'd sheltered from the cyclone. The grandmother told Nahkala that you must have really cared for the boy, otherwise you wouldn't have been so loving towards him.'

'That's because he's easy to love, but surely there's someone else who can be his guardian?'

'Apparently, Nee-Ty has no other blood relatives and for a Tarparniian child to be adopted into another family can be…well, it can be very difficult.'

'But I thought you said the verbal contract was binding between two clans? That it was considered a dishonour not to accept the adoption?'

'And sometimes, when there are no other living relatives, it's done more as a formality and the child is treated as a poor relative, not given true status within the adoptive family and does tend to struggle to find his place in the world. There is still no country in the world that has pure equality, Cora.'

'True. So if Nee-Ty was handed over to another family or village, he might be ridiculed?'

'The possibility is high, especially as, from what we can gather, he's already been subjected to such behaviour by his own village. It was only because his grandmother was a matriarch that he was afforded any sort of…pleasantries after the death of his parents but now that she has passed away he's considered an outcast. His village elders are saying that they don't want him.'

'Oh, the poor thing.' Cora stared at Nee-Ty, remembering how he'd told Archer that he'd been sent to find berries just before the cyclone had been due to hit. Who had sent him? Why had they sent him? Had it been a joke but being so young Nee-Ty hadn't understood the undertones and had, therefore, gone off to find berries, only to discover a heavy storm approaching? Even then, the little boy had headed for the caves, proving that he was quite intelligent.

Cora covered her hands with her face. 'What am I supposed to do?'

'I don't know,' Melora stated.

'What we need to do,' a deep male voice said, and both women looked up to see Archer walking towards them, the torch he held giving him an ethereal glow, 'is to begin the burial arrangements for Nee-Ty's grandmother. The Tarparnese consider the first three hours after a person's death to be the most crucial. If proper rituals are not performed, his grandmother's spirit might never find true peace and could haunt all those who lived in the village with her.'

'Which none of them will want,' Cora tried not to grumble, as she carefully stood, stretching out her cramped limbs. 'What about Nee-Ty? Do we tell him about his grandmother's death? Does he attend the funeral?'

Archer shook his head. 'Generally, Tarparnian children are shielded from death until they come of age, at around twelve. They are taught, however, about *Jeh-la-derri*.'

'The place the spirits go?' she asked, still trying to get her head around a lot of the Tarparnian traditions.

'Exactly.'

'OK.' Cora closed her eyes for a moment, picturing the smile on Nee-Ty's face when they'd arrived at the village. He'd been happy to be seeing his grandmother again. Now she was gone. Cora sighed and opened her eyes, looking at Archer. 'How are the negotiations going?'

'There's still a lot to be discussed.' He massaged his temples. 'But first things first.' He crooked his elbow towards Cora. 'Better hang on to me. The ground can get a little uneven.'

'I'll check on the kids,' Melora stated, before leaving them.

Cora said goodbye to her friend and slipped her hand around Archer's arm, too exhausted to fight the warm tingles that gently flooded her body at the contact. 'What am I supposed to do?' she asked.

'Just stay by me. You'll be fine.'

She sighed knowing that if she wasn't able to go and get some sleep, leaning against Archer might be the next best thing. 'Thanks for the vote of confidence.'

They walked carefully towards the area reserved for the burial rituals, which was set apart from the rest of the village. The area was surrounded by flaming torches, with Cora and Archer being the only non-Tarparniians there.

She wasn't quite sure how she managed to get through the next three hours. She was still exhausted from the cyclone and medical emergency, and the last thing she needed was to focus on these rituals. Fatigue had definitely arrived, however, and being a doctor meant working all hours and learning different ways to battle sluggishness, especially when it counted most.

'Does anyone know her name?' Nahkala asked, and several people shrugged their shoulders, many saying that everyone in the village only called her Grandmother or Wise One.

'Uh…' Cora remarked tentatively, and Nahkala encouraged her to speak up. 'When I first found Nee-Ty, he was calling out Ni-Kaowa. Could that be her name?'

Nahkala's eyes widened at this news and she sadly shook her head. 'She was not his grandmother, she was his great-grandmother. Ni-Kaowa means great-grandmother. Nee-Ty is her son's son's son.'

'Does that matter?'

'Yes. It means that Nee-Ty is the very last of his clan and as such is more alone than before, the lines of succession having been broken for two generations before him.'

Cora was still unsure of exactly what that meant but tears of sadness pricked at her eyes as she tried to contemplate what it must be like to be buried without anyone knowing your name. How lonely, and yet there were a lot of people around them, attending to the ceremonial needs for this wise woman, Nee-Ty's Ni-Kaowa.

As she stood there, trying to keep her eyes open, she wasn't sure just how much longer she could last. Her breathing started to deepen and she was positive she'd dozed off for a second as she couldn't remember what had just been said. Her mind was incapable of translating any of the Tarparnese so she simply let it wash over her.

'Whoa. Steady there.' Archer's deep voice sounded near her ears and his firm arm came around her shoulders. Cora snapped her eyes open and looked up at him, the glow from the torches casting strange shadows over his face.

'I think we can leave soon.'

'But isn't there more? The funeral pyre?'

'You don't need to be here for that.' A moment later, after one of the village elders had called out something to the spirits, Archer leaned close again. 'I'll take you back now.'

As the rest of the group prepared the pyre, Archer and Cora walked back towards the village. She was grateful that he kept his arm about her shoulders, steadying her as she stumbled several times not only due to lack of vision but to her tiredness. Amazingly, he didn't smell bad, especially given the day they'd had.

Instead, there was still that subtle hint of spice about him and combined with the feel of his arm around her it wasn't at all surprising that she found herself wishing she'd get to spend more time with him.

'Who's going to tell Nee-Ty what's happened?' she asked, when they reached the outskirts of the village.

'I'm not sure.'

'I'd like to be there.'

'OK. I'll let Nahkala know but they won't talk to him until the guardianship issue has been resolved.'

'Uh-huh.'

'Are you even aware of what I'm saying?'

'Uh-huh.' His warm laughter rumbled through her and she sighed. 'You have a nice laugh.'

'You really don't know me well enough to be giving me compliments like that.' The laughter disappeared and there was a slight growl to his words, as though he really didn't want her liking him at all, and she couldn't help but wonder why. Why wouldn't anyone like to be liked?

Before she knew it, they were standing in front

of purple hut and Archer was releasing her from his arms. 'Go, Cora. Sleep. I'll fix everything.'

'OK.' She sighed once more, then turned and headed into the purple hut, trying to keep her eyes open long enough to make sure she didn't stumble over people who were already sound asleep. Thankfully, she found a spare sleeping mat already laid out. Whether or not it had been assigned to her, she was past caring. She lay down, not bothering to loosen her clothing or even take off her shoes. Instead, she pulled the light blanket over herself and smiled as visions of Archer entered her mind. Archer holding her close, angling his head towards her, finally claiming her lips in an earth-shattering kiss. She sighed and embraced the fantastic dream.

When Cora finally awoke the next morning it was to find herself alone in the hut. For a moment she was rather disorientated but then everything came flooding back: the aftermath of the cyclone; the busy clinics; the death of Nee-Ty's great-grandmother.

'Nee-Ty!' She sat bolt upright, hoping that Nahkala and the other elders hadn't told the boy anything about his grandmother's death because Cora had really wanted to be there to comfort Nee-Ty. She flicked back the blanket, annoyed when her feet became tangled in the end of it.

She was still wearing her boots, still fully clothed from the events of the past few days. She felt gritty and grimy but scrambled to her feet and rushed for the door to the hut, sliding it open, her eyes squinting against the bright sun.

'What time is it?' she murmured, and why had she been left to sleep for so long? The clinic tents were already set up, with the majority of PMA staff hard at work as they tended to people who were lining up, waiting for treatment. Everywhere she looked patients were talking, children were crying, others were sitting down, not moving much at all.

She wanted to help, and she would, but first she needed to find Nee-Ty, to make sure he was all right. It would be difficult for him to accept the truth of his grandmother's death, especially when he'd been so excited to see her yesterday.

'Ahh. Sleeping beauty has awoken!' Archer's jovial tone made her look up to see him walking towards her.

'Where's Nee-Ty? Have they told him about his grandmother yet?'

Archer shook his head and she immediately relaxed her shoulders, letting out a huge sigh of relief. 'Thank goodness.'

'But they are ready. That's why I was coming to get you.'

'Yes, I'm sorry I overslept.' Suddenly feeling rather self-conscious about her appearance, especially as she hadn't changed her clothes since she'd first met Archer almost two days ago, Cora raked her fingers through her hair, hoping she didn't have any weird bits sticking up at odd angles.

'Don't worry about it.' He held out his hand, indicating the path before them. 'Shall we?'

'Thanks.' She knew the path led to Nahkala's hut and as they drew closer, for some reason, her legs began to feel like they were made of lead. She stopped just outside and wrung her hands. 'This isn't going to be easy.' Her words were soft, as though she were talking to herself more than him, but she was aware that Archer had heard her.

'Giving bad news is never easy, but to a child?

Does he even comprehend what death really means? That because of Ni'Kaowa's death his life is changed for ever?'

Archer spread his arms wide then let them fall lifelessly back to his sides.

'Earlier this morning, I was walking past the green hut and I found Nee-Ty sitting patiently on the step.' He shook his head. 'When I asked him what he was doing, he told me it was what he would do every day. He'd go out and pick berries, doing his best not to squash them, and once he'd delivered them to the women, if none of them gave him another job to do, he'd return and sit on the front steps of his hut, waiting for someone to give him a job or tell him to do something. His Ni-Kaowa would often be busy with settling disputes or organising new regimes within the village and he would be left to wait.

'He told me he was good at waiting and some-times he would be so good that he'd sit there all day long, just watching everyone else go about their business. Sometimes he would eat the ber-ries off the bush before he started picking them because that might be all the food he was al-lowed to eat for that day.'

Archer's eyes were filled with sadness as he related this information to her. Even though Archer felt uncomfortable around children, he still cared.

'No. Oh, no. The poor baby. What sort of life has he had so far?' She shook her head. 'And what sort of future has been decided for him?'

Archer opened his mouth to inform her but the door to the hut slid open and Nahkala stood there, staring at the two of them.

'You are ready?' she asked, and Cora wanted to say that, no, she wasn't ready. That life wasn't fair, that the fate of this little boy shouldn't depend on a village vote. Why couldn't Nee-Ty simply be wanted? Needed? Loved?

'Yes. We are ready,' Archer said, and placed his hand in the small of Cora's back, urging her forward into the hut. The instant Nee-Ty saw her he rushed forward, his mask still held firmly in his hands. Now it was the only thing that connected him to his roots. Cora picked him up and hugged him close, kissing his cheek and trying to hold back the tears that sprang to her eyes. She forced a smile and sat in the seat Nahkala offered.

'We shall begin.' Nahkala spoke with quiet authority as Cora glanced at the other people gathered here. Along with Nahkala and Daniel, there were two elders from Nee-Ty's village and two elders from Nahkala's village.

'One of our teachings,' the wise woman was saying, 'is that we do not show our children the face of death. They are taught about our beliefs from a young age and Nee-Ty he may only comprehend the name of the place: Jeh'lah-derri.'

Cora realised belatedly that Nahkala was explaining things more for her benefit than anyone else's because at that name, Jeh'lah-derri, Nee-Ty stopped playing with his mask and sat up straighter in her arms.

'Jeh'lah-derri?' He spoke each syllable clearly, turned wide eyes towards Cora. As she looked down into the little boy's face, her heart broke and tears instantly sprang to her eyes.

'Ni-Kaowa...' she began, but her voice choked on a sob. To her surprise, she felt Archer place his hand on her shoulder, offering comfort. Nee-Ty stared up at him as Archer picked up where Cora had left off, softly and quietly telling the little boy that his Ni-Kaowa had gone to Jeh'lah-derri.

Even as Archer was speaking, Nee-Ty's breathing increased as pure sadness overwhelmed him. His lower lip wobbled and his eyes filled with tears and, seeing him like this, Cora felt she could contain her sadness no longer. It was not for the wise old woman that she cried but for the little boy who was all alone.

As soon as Cora's tears started so did Nee-Ty's, and she hugged him close. 'I'm so sorry,' she whispered over and over again, rubbing his back, letting him know that she was there for him. She didn't care about the elders in the room, whether they approved of her tears or not. She knew what it was like to lose people you loved and it didn't matter whether you were old or young, the pain was immense.

She also knew what it was like to lose a future because before her accident she'd planned on one very specific future but that dream had been taken away from her. She'd had no option and the surgery had changed her world for ever.

Archer pressed a handkerchief into her hand and she quickly dabbed at her eyes, not bothering with Nee-Ty's as he'd buried his face beneath her shoulder, his tears absorbed by her shirt.

'I do understand this is a difficult situation,' Nahkala remarked softly after a few minutes had passed. 'However, there is still much to do. We must finalise the transfer of Nee-Ty's heritage from his village to mine.'

Cora looked up at this. 'Pardon?'

'Nee-Ty will become a permanent member of my village. The elders here will watch over him, take responsibility for him. There are two families who have come forward to accept him.'

'He'll live with both of them?' Cora was perplexed and she dabbed at her eyes once more before blowing her nose.

'It is expensive to take on the child of another man,' Nahkala explained politely. 'Overseeing the matter and sharing the cost is one of the ways for a village to help out.'

Cora shook her head, her thoughts whirring as she imagined Nee-Ty sitting on the step of a hut, waiting all day long for someone to give him a job, for someone to find a use for him, for someone to hold him, need him, love him. It wasn't that difficult. He was very easy to love!

'Wait a second. Just wait.' She held up one hand, the little boy's tears having subsided to a whimper, followed by several short hiccups. Whenever she held him like this, she felt such a sense of…rightness. It was right for her to be with Nee-Ty. She had obstacles in her life that it would take a miracle to overcome but perhaps her miracle was being handed to her on a silver platter.

'Cora?' Nahkala was watching her closely— as was Archer.

'Cora?' There was a hint of warning in his tone. 'Don't.'

'Why not?' she asked him, her eyes starting to fill with delight at the prospect of actually accepting the guardianship of the boy.

'Because you haven't thought this through.' He spread his arms wide. 'Because it's too life-changing for Nee-Ty and for a whole lot of other reasons.'

'So he's just supposed to spend the rest of his life waiting on the step of a hut?' She shook her head for emphasis. 'No.'

'What are you saying?' Archer stood and stared at her, his hands firmly at his side, in that darned military stance that was starting to drive her crazy. Why couldn't he see that this was the right thing to do? Why did he always have to live his life by the rule book? 'That you'll take Nee-Ty? That you'll accept the adoption? That you'll take him back to Australia with you? Become his full-time parent? That's not going to be easy.'

'You forget, Archer. I have siblings. A lot of them. I was seventeen when my baby sister was born and I helped my stepmother a lot—we all did, so I'm not as naive as you might think when it comes to raising a child. Besides, there are some occasions in life where a person is challenged, seriously challenged, and how they adapt, how they cope with this challenge can determine not only a different course for their future but also change them deep inside.' She placed her hand over her heart. 'And it's a change that can help sculpt the rest of their life.'

She sighed heavily and raked a hand through her hair, not caring how it looked. 'The point is—plain and simple—that I love Nee-Ty. I love him like I love one of my siblings and I will never leave my siblings and I will never leave Nee-Ty.'

'But is it right to take him out of his environment, his culture?' Archer persisted. 'Or are you planning to move permanently to Tarparnii?'

'Think of the new opportunities he can be given, as well as maintaining a firm grounding in his original traditions.' She indicated Daniel, sitting opposite her, listening intently to all that was said. 'Daniel is half-Tarparniian and was raised across two different cultures and he's managed to turn out very well, as have his children.'

'Thank you,' Daniel murmured, and received a glare from Archer for his troubles.

'What's to say the same can't happen for Nee-Ty? That, being raised across two cultures, he'll turn out just as balanced?'

'That is a valid question,' Nahkala remarked, chiming in. She'd been quietly translating to the other Tarparniians in the room, so everyone was appraised of this recent turn of events. 'Why do you want Nee-Ty? The reason deep down?'

Cora took a deep breath, dropped a kiss on Nee-Ty's head and tightened her arms around him. 'He's all alone.' She closed her eyes and swallowed before looking directly at Archer. 'And so am I.'

'What?' Archer was stunned.

'Cora. Are you absolutely sure?' Nahkala spoke clearly. 'This is a huge step.'

She nodded. 'I'm used to taking huge steps, I'm used to adventure, and being guardian of Nee-Ty will definitely be an adventure.'

'You're not thinking straight at all.' Archer threw his arms in the air.

'Archer does raise a valid point,' Nahkala continued, then turned to everyone present. 'We will stop now and come together later. Please,' she urged everyone present, her gaze resting especially on Cora, 'consider wisely.'

'That's good advice.' Archer's words were spoken in a low voice but Cora heard. She levelled a glare at him before turning and stalking from the hut. 'Seriously, Cora,' he stated, and it was only then she realised he'd followed her out. 'Think about what you're doing. This is a little boy's life. You're going to change it for ever.'

'So why is that a bad thing?' She stopped walking so suddenly he almost bumped into her. Even though he was taller, she stood her ground, lifting her chin with defiance, her shoulders firmly set. 'I'm offering Nee-Ty the chance at a proper life, to be loved. Everyone deserves to be loved. What do you have against that?'

Archer clenched his jaw and jammed his hands into his pockets. He hadn't been loved. No one had come to *his* rescue but he couldn't tell Cora that. It was true, what she was offering Nee-Ty was the chance at an amazing life. It wasn't odd for PMA staff to adopt orphans from Tarparnii. In fact, he had quite a few friends who had done just that: offering the opportunity of being raised across two cultures. But his friends hadn't been taking on the role of a single parent.

'I don't have anything against that,' he finally answered when she continued to stare at him. 'It's just that as a single parent you…well, I don't think you truly realise what a change that will mean to your life.'

'I'll work it out. I'm good at doing that, plus I have fami—'

'Family support,' he finished for her. He looked down at the ground and exhaled harshly.

'Why are you so against me doing this?' Her words weren't as brisk as before and when he met her gaze once more Cora shrugged her shoulders and spread her arms wide. 'Is it because *you* can't offer the same? That you feel backed into a corner?'

Archer wanted to tell her that was exactly how he was feeling, that she already knew he was uncomfortable around children so why was she pressuring him into stepping forward and agreeing to become Nee-Ty's co-guardian? That's when it dawned on him that she *wasn't* pressuring him. He was pressuring himself. Archer shook his head and opened his mouth to say something but clamped it shut again. Then he turned on his heel and stalked away.

Cora watched him go, feeling as though she'd just been put through the wringer for no real reason. She was trying to do something nice, *wanting* to do something nice. She loved Nee-Ty and she knew with all her heart that she could give him a much better life than he could ever have here. Surely Archer could see that? She wasn't trying to be self-important but perhaps he couldn't and the reason he couldn't was because he really didn't know her that well at all. Sure, they'd shared some very intense experiences but that didn't mean they understood each other.

As Cora headed off to reflect some more on

her decision, knowing there was no way she was going to change her mind, she hoped Archer was doing the same, that he would see in her the qualities of a woman who not only knew the right course of action but wasn't afraid to take it.

Why she was hoping to garner Archer's good opinion was another thought that came to mind? Was it that she didn't like him to think badly of her? That she had to show him, convince him, that she was right? Cora shook her head, pushing thoughts of Archer Wild aside and focusing on Nee-Ty.

When one of the elders came to bring her back to Nahkala's hut Cora was ready with her logical reasons as to why this course of action was right. She met Archer's gaze as she entered the hut, hoping to see understanding in his eyes, but instead all she saw was indifference. The discussion commenced, with Cora stating logical and thought-provoking reasons as to why she would make a good guardian, and her words seemed to satisfy the elders. Archer kept quiet.

She turned and faced the elders of Nahkala's village, her head bowed in reverence of their position. 'And, finally, I hope you will all agree that your village will become Nee-Ty's ancestral home. It's important to me that he understands his heritage.'

Nahkala's answer was to open her arms and wrap them around Cora and Nee-Ty. 'You have chosen wisely,' she stated. 'And. of course, this village will now become Nee-Ty's ancestral home. His mask will remain in my care until he is of age, when he shall return for his ceremony.'

'Wait. Wait!' Archer held up his hands, the stiff military stance broken due to his complete bewilderment and frustration. 'Cora, you haven't explained what you meant before. When you said Nee-Ty was all alone and that you were, too. What is that supposed to mean? You're a triplet. You have siblings, as you've continually pointed out to me. So how can you be "all alone"?'

Cora nodded and drew in a calming breath. 'Yes, I have siblings…siblings who are able to have children of their own.' She spoke softly and it took a moment for her words to sink in.

'Your accident. The pelvic fracture.' Archer whispered the words.

'That's right.' Cora glanced down at Nee-Ty then back at Archer. 'I can't ever have children.'

CHAPTER SIX

ARCHER TRUDGED SLOWLY through the scrubland, heading towards his favourite place around Nah-kala's village. It was a place he and Daniel had found when they'd been younger and it was a place he'd often delighted in visiting again every time he was back in Tarparnii.

The watering hole, a place where many of the villagers came to swim and relax, was close by. The fresh stream of water was the reason why Nahkala's village had survived in its present location for many years. But a little further up from the watering hole, where the river curved, heading into a denser area of scrub land, was his perfect place.

A tree, very similar to a weeping willow but one that was native to Tarparnii, still dipped its wide overhanging branches into the edge of the stream. Archer pushed aside the branches and made his way into the secret place…the place of serenity.

He had much to think about, especially given the past seventy-two hours. A few days ago he'd never heard the name Cora Wilton in his life and now she seemed to be a constant thought, both one he kept wanting to push to the back of his mind and one he wanted to unravel. He wanted to figure out what it was about her that seemed to entice him, to draw him close, to confuse his usually well-ordered world.

The woman was gorgeous, there was no doubting that, and perhaps from the first moment he'd looked into her eyes, pushing her hair back from her face, she'd managed to connect the two of them with invisible bonds. She'd done something, because ever since then he'd experienced the overwhelming urge to protect her—no matter what.

Where he'd thought he'd been doing the right thing, securing the future of little Nee-Ty with a Tarparniian family, a family that would indeed give him the traditional up bringing the little one deserved, Cora had overturned that decision without any consultation. Yes, she'd admitted that she wouldn't be able to have children but was adopting a three-year-old Tarparniian boy the way to rectify that?

Archer shook his head, sure he would never understand women. After the upbringing he'd had, he'd planned never to have any children. Georgie, his lovely wife, had agreed to this and had thrown herself into being the perfect army wife, travelling with him, organising charity events with the other army wives. She'd been a giver...and he'd taken. He'd taken everything she'd had to give, which, in his mind, had made him no better than his selfish father.

He closed his eyes, remembering how he'd done everything he could in order to gain his father's acceptance, his approval, to make him proud of his son—but it had never happened. He'd bowed to his father's way of doing things, completing everything his father had asked, and for what? For pain. For mortification. For fear of trusting and giving to others because in the end they really didn't care at all. Archer had learned the hard way that to try and please others, to do what you thought others expected of you, could only lead to heartbreak. All he'd wanted had been an 'I'm proud of you, son,' but it had never happened.

It made him feel sick to his stomach when he reflected on the way Georgie had clearly been trying to please him too. She was a giver and she'd given him her all. Had she done it because no one had ever taught her how to receive? Why hadn't he realised that her love for him had been driven from the desire to make sure he was always happy?

He'd wanted to go trekking to different countries, and so she'd willingly gone with him. He'd wanted to go mountain climbing, abseiling, skydiving, and Georgie had gone willingly. Thinking back, he had often seen that look of dread on her face, especially when she'd been about to do her first ever tandem skydive. He'd tried to encourage her by telling her to face her fear, to conquer it, to let go…and she had. He'd been so proud of her, with the way she'd pushed through whatever reservations she'd had. She'd trusted him completely, and he'd let her down.

He hadn't returned her trust. Hadn't stopped to consider what it was *she* wanted from their life together. It wasn't until the white-water rafting event that she'd finally given voice to her inner concerns.

'I'm not sure I should go,' she'd told him, as he'd gathered the gear they would need for the adventure. 'I'm not feeling the best.'

'It's just nerves,' he'd replied. 'You've conquered them before.' Archer had crossed to her side, put both his hands on her shoulders and looked into her eyes. 'We've spent all our lives following other people's rules, Georgie. You've done everything your parents ever wanted; you've been the perfect daughter—even agreeing to marry me.' He'd pulled a face, distorting his features, and she'd laughed.

'But I love you,' Georgie had insisted, and had stood on tiptoe to kiss him. 'I like spending time with you, doing the things that make you happy.'

'Which is why you're going to *love* white-water rafting: the thrill; the adrenaline; the freedom!' He'd punched a fist in the air and she'd laughed again but this time there'd been a thread of nervousness to her laughter.

Why hadn't he noticed before? Why hadn't he listened to her and agreed that she could stay home? Why, why, why? But he knew that no amount of whys were going to bring Georgie back to life. Their white-water rafting adventure had been their last adventure together, Georgie having been swept overboard, her harness snapping due to the ferocity of the rapids, and by the time they'd reached her, it had been too late.

They'd been married for less than a year and after their white-water rafting adventure they'd been supposed to attend Daniel and Melora's wedding. Instead of taking part in the Tarparniian *par'Mach* ceremony to bind Daniel to his beautiful wife, Archer had returned to England to arrange Georgie's funeral. Then he'd applied for an honourable discharge from the army and joined the permanent medical team in Tarparnii, moving from village to village, going where he was needed, giving to others but keeping himself separate.

Until he'd met Cora.

Was Cora the same as Georgie? Doing what she thought was right in order to please others? Didn't she realise that taking on the care of Nee-Ty wasn't just a short-term event—that this would be for the rest of her life? Yes, she had a bigger family than him and, yes, she definitely cared about the little boy, but this was a permanent change. The adoption of a child.

After Cora had accepted the adoption, carrying Nee-Ty from the hut, Archer had paced around Nahkala's small room while waiting for everyone else to leave.

'This is ridiculous,' he'd told the village matriarch. 'Cora doesn't know the ways of your country.'

'Like you do?' Nahkala had asked.

'You know I'm not equipped to take care of a young boy.'

'I understand the thought of parenthood strikes fear into your heart.' Nahkala had placed her hand over Archer's heart and looked up at him. 'You are a good man, Archer Wild. I have seen your face with many expressions, I have seen your heart constricted with pain and joy. This event has occurred. A child has been offered to you, his young life waiting to be guided by your experience. I do not consider this to be accidental, or that you are bonded in this task with Cora. The grandmother chose wisely.'

'But, Nahkala—' He stopped, breaking off his words as the wise woman had looked up at him with such belief, her expression indicating that all was indeed right with this strange situation.

'You like adventures, Archer,' she'd said, patting her hand on his heart. 'Do not allow fear to stop you from taking a different one, an adventure of the soul. Cora. She will help you, Archer, but only if you allow her.'

And that was why he'd come to sit and think. Could he let Cora into his carefully constructed world? Would it be as Nahkala had said? Daniel's mother was a wise woman and he'd never known her to be wrong before, but was it possible that he and Cora could maintain guardianship of a little three-year-old boy?

He'd asked Cora the other day when her contract was up with PMA and she'd told him she'd be home in time for Christmas. That was only a few weeks away. Would she take the boy with her? Would the love she clearly felt for the child be enough to assist him through the culture shock?

'He needs someone there, someone who can understand his dialect, understand the world from which he's come and to help build a bridge to where he might end up.' Archer spoke the words out loud, a new determination flooding through him.

'Hello? Is someone there?'

He knew that voice, that lovely sweet voice. It was the voice of the woman he'd dreamed about last night when he'd finally managed to get some sleep. It was the voice of the woman who was never far from his thoughts. It was the voice of the woman he most needed to talk to.

'Cora?'

'Archer? Where are you?'

'Inside the tree.' His words made her laugh and the pretty sound blended perfectly with the soothing sounds of Mother Nature.

'What? *Inside* the tree?' She chuckled. 'How is that possible?'

Archer stood and walked to the edge of the branches, pulling them back to see her standing close to him on the path, looking around earnestly in search of him. 'Over here,' he called, and when her gaze finally met his the smile she bestowed on him made his heart beat faster. What was it about this woman that seemed to send his hormones into overdrive?

'How do I get there?'

He was quick to walk over to the nearby rocks and hold up a hand to her so she could climb down safely.

'Thank you.' She accepted his help. 'I think this is where we came in. You helping me to climb over rocks and boulders.'

'At least the weather is a little different today,' he remarked, as he led the way back to his secret tree.

'How did you find this place?' Cora waited for him to separate the branches for her before she ducked beneath the overhanging foliage. 'Oh, my goodness. This is lovely.'

Archer couldn't help the smile that came naturally to his lips at her reaction. 'Daniel and I found it when we were just kids.'

'Ooh. Is this, like, your secret hiding place?'

'Something like that. The canopy seemed bigger back then, and as you can see there's quite a bit of space. We'd pretend we were visiting an alien planet or that we were…superheroes.' Archer was surprised that it didn't feel strange to talk to Cora about his childhood.

'Aha! So you *do* have superhero genes. I knew

it.' She sat down, resting her back against the trunk.

Archer sat next to her and shook his head. 'That was a long time ago.'

'And yet you still come here.' Her words were wistful. 'I like that.'

He shrugged. 'It's a good place to think.'

'Oh? And what have you been thinking about today?'

'You.' The word was out before he could stop it. Cora raised her eyebrows, a small concerned smile hovering about her exceedingly kissable mouth.

'Is that a good thing?'

'It's a...confusing thing,' he confessed.

'Because I'm accepting the guardianship of Nee-Ty?'

'Yes.' Archer shoved his fingers through his hair and stood, unable to sit still. 'I understand, when you say that you can't have children, why this might seem like the perfect solution, but is it? To be raising a child alone?'

Cora stared at him for a long moment before looking down at the ground. 'I won't be alone.'

'I know. You have family, but, Cora—'

'Archer, I spent most of my eighteenth year in and out of hospital. I had a bladder rupture, busted intestines and my uterus was a mess. They managed to save one ovary but even then, the only way I'd ever be able to have a natural-born child is through surrogacy, and while both my sisters instantly offered to carry my child, the possibility of it all succeeding, of a fertilised egg adhering to the surrogate mother...' She spread her hands wide. 'You know the odds as well as I do and, yes, there have been many technological advances in this field but I had to face the prospect that I would never become a mother.'

She sighed and shook her head. 'My sister Jasmine was only a few months old when I had the accident. Two of my closest friends died in the same car crash and I was trapped in the car for almost five hours.'

His jaw clenched at her words but he didn't interrupt with the usual platitudes, for which she was grateful. 'For years I've tried my best to accept my situation. It's one of the reasons why I came to Tarparnii, why I started working with PMA. I decided that if I wasn't going to be having children of my own then what was the point in settling down in a nine-to-five family clinic, treating other pregnant women, looking after their children, day in, day out?'

'But you see pregnant women here. You treat children here.'

'Yes, but you know as well as I do that here it's different. Their lives are different. Sure, I saw a child the other day who had shoved a small stone up his nose and in the past I've removed a plastic toy from another little boy's nose, but here my help really does seem to make a difference.'

'So why not keep doing that? Why take on the responsibility of raising a child? You can be like me and join the Tarparnii medical team full time, you can live here, work here, helping those who need it most.'

Cora shook her head, her expression one of sadness because there was no way Archer could ever understand what it was like to be a part of a big family, to have the connection of sisters and brothers, sharing and caring for each other. 'My family is in Australia and I love them, too. Live here? All year round?' She shook her head again. 'Not possible.'

'I guess as I don't have siblings, I'll never understand that.'

'But what about Daniel? He's like a brother to you. Nahkala is like a mother to you. How do you feel when you see them? When Daniel and Melora return to Tarparnii. How do you feel when you see them?'

Archer put his hands on his hips and regarded her with a confused expression. 'I'm happy to see them.'

'And do you and Daniel ever come here…' she spread her arms wide, indicating their present surroundings '…and reminisce about old times, about the fun you used to have?'

'Rarely, but—yes.'

'Are you able to just share a look with him and he knows exactly what you're thinking?'

The confusion started to lift from his brow as Cora continued thinking aloud. 'When you have an issue you need to talk through, who do you trust to give you wise counsel? Who, when you need them most, will drop everything to be by your side?'

He could think of a few people who would do

that for him but Daniel would be first in line. 'But that's friendship.'

'Exactly. My siblings are my closest friends. I love hanging out with them, supporting them, helping them, and I get the same in return. They're friends who will never leave you, even if you have a fight or disagreement.'

'Huh.'

'And that's what I want for Nee-Ty, too. He should be given the chance to grow up in a loving and caring environment, to have people around him who will support him, teach him, guide him.' She stood and clutched her hands to her chest. 'He fills a gaping hole within me, just as I can fill the hole in his life.'

Cora took a few steps towards Archer, desperate to help him to understand how she felt about this situation. 'I've tried, several times, to fill this hole with relationships that didn't go anywhere. I was dating a fellow medical student for over a year, thinking that he was "the one", that I'd finally found a way to satisfy the need I had to have just one thing to be mine.'

She shrugged and continued to move slowly towards him. 'I know that might sound insane, especially when I already have so much, and it's not that I don't love being a triplet—I do— but sometimes you just want something that belongs to you…not to you *and* your sisters.' Cora sighed. 'But relationships were the wrong place to look. Of course, I realised that once I'd had my heart broken a few times.'

Archer nodded as though he understood what she was saying. 'So you turned to adventure and helping others?'

'Yes.'

'So did I.' His hands were still on his hips, his body language far from the stiff military stance he usually adopted. 'For completely different reasons, of course,' he added.

'I think…' She continued to move towards him, drawing closer and closer, half expecting him to take a step away or to cross his arms over his chest in a defensive manner, erecting walls between them, but he did neither. 'When you lose something important or an event happens in your life that robs you of your envisioned future, you fill it with things that can at least make a difference in someone's life.'

'Exactly.'

Cora was now standing right in front of him, her arms by her sides, looking up at him, the look in her deep brown eyes hypnotising him. 'Archer?'

'Mmm?' He dropped his gaze to take in her parted lips, lips he wasn't sure he could resist kissing. Several times since they'd met they'd been this close and each time he'd wanted nothing more than to lower his head to see precisely what it was that existed between them.

This time he wanted to follow through on that desire and when he reached forward to tuck her hair behind her ear, Cora's breath rushed out, as though she'd been holding it, waiting for him to make the first move.

'What is this?' he whispered, cupping her cheek with his hand, his thumb gently caressing her soft skin.

'I don't know.' She swallowed and placed her hands on his chest, gasping with delight at the contact. 'But I really want to find out.'

'So do I.'

With that, he lowered his head, desperate to finally get some answers.

CHAPTER SEVEN

NO SOONER HAD his lips pressed against the softness of hers, his senses drinking in the subtle sweetness of everything that was Cora, than his satellite phone rang.

Groaning with impatience, Archer pulled back, staring down into her upturned face, her closed eyelids slowly opening as he wrenched the phone free from his pocket.

'Wild here.'

He listened to whoever was on the other end of the line while still completely captivated by the woman before him.

'Copy that,' he remarked a moment later. 'I'll be there soon.' He disconnected the call and put the phone back in his pocket but didn't make any move to continue where they'd left off. 'I have to go.'

'Problem?'

'Patient has a complication.'

Cora nodded and bit the corner of her lip, unsure what to do or say next. 'OK.' They both stood there, staring at each other. She shifted back a little, needing a bit of distance between them. 'Thank you,' she finally ventured.

'For the kiss?' Archer shoved his hands into his pockets, pleased that she seemed as uncomfortable as him.

'And for listening. I appreciate it.'

He nodded. 'It has helped me to understand your actions better.'

'Good.'

He needed to go, needed to reassess his patient and, more than likely, needed to return to Theatre to address the complication. What he didn't need to do was to stand here, gazing into Cora's beautiful face, wondering whether or not he should kiss her once more before leaving. This was so unlike him. He hated being so indecisive. He dragged in a breath, hoping to try and settle his jumbled thoughts, but instead all he succeeded in doing was breathing in her fresh, floral scent.

'You smell so good.' The words were out of his

mouth before he could stop them. Cora gasped and stared at him before nodding.

'I had a shower.' She continued to stare at him, her gaze flicking from his eyes to his mouth and back again, her breathing increasing, her lips parted. She not only smelled good, she looked so alluring, her fringe still falling forward into her eyes. He clenched his hands into fists, trying to fight the urge to gather her into his arms and kiss her properly, but she deserved more attention, deserved more than a few stolen kisses before he headed off to Theatre.

'Uh…Cora—' he began, about to suggest they try and find some time later on to discuss things in greater detail, when she covered the distance between them in a few short strides, stood on tiptoe and pressed her mouth firmly to his.

His hands instantly came to her waist, gathering her closer and supporting her as his mouth meshed with hers. How was it possible that she seemed to fit so perfectly against him? How was it possible that he was even kissing another woman…and enjoying every moment of it? How was it possible for him to put her aside and head to Theatre? It wasn't.

The flavours of her mouth were as addictive as her sweet scent and he simply wanted to stay here, in this moment, for as long as he could.

'Archer.' She whispered his name against his mouth and he kissed her once more. 'You need to—'

He stopped her words with another kiss, knowing the truth of their situation, but just for once, just for one wacky moment, wanting to ignore all sense and reason.

'Go and see your patient.'

Archer exhaled harshly and buried his face in her neck, delighted when the action caused her to giggle. 'I'm ticklish there,' she confessed, lifting her shoulder in order to guard the area. 'Now I have goose-bumps.' She laughed again.

'You have the sweetest laugh.' He reluctantly released her from his hold and brushed her hair behind her ear.

'Thank you.' She smiled brightly up at him. 'How about I walk back with you? I could even assist in Theatre if necessary.'

'No, it's fine.' Archer stepped back, shaking his head slightly. 'You stay and enjoy your walk. This area is quite lovely at this time of day.'

He clenched his jaw and shoved his hands into his pockets again. Cora wasn't sure whether it was to stop himself from touching her again or whether something else was wrong. There was a slight briskness to his words, as though he was already regretting having given in to the urge to kiss her.

'OK. I'll do that.' She smiled up at him, both of them standing there, staring at each other again, neither of them moving. This was not good. She knew he needed to go and review his patient, as did he, but the tension and pheromones were still zinging in the air around them.

'Well, all righty, then.' Cora finally managed to move. 'Let's both go our separate ways.' She walked towards the overhanging foliage but Archer was there before her, holding the branches apart, sunlight flooding into the secluded area. 'I hope everything goes well with your patient.'

'Bunda.' He offered the patient's name and she nodded as her eyes adjusted to the change in light.

'Ah, yes. He wasn't looking too good earlier on.'

'That's why I came out here with the phone,' he said, patting his pocket.

'OK.' Why was it so difficult for them to part? Why did Cora want to accompany him back to the village, to continue spending time with him, even if that meant being in Theatre? Surely, given the events of the past few days, they hadn't already developed a co-dependence on each other?

'Enjoy your stroll,' he said, as he walked towards the rocks.

'I will.' She smiled and headed in the opposite direction from him. 'I'll see you later on.'

'Count on it,' he remarked, and with that he finally turned his back on her and headed off towards the village. Cora took three steps down the path before stopping and watching Archer until he was completely out of sight.

She turned and headed towards the stream, her thoughts rushing faster than the sparkling clear water. So far today she'd inherited a three-year-old boy and kissed the man she couldn't seem to stop thinking about. What it all meant she had no clue. Thrusting her hands into her hair, Cora closed her eyes and shook her head. How on earth had her life become so complicated so quickly?

* * *

Cora had to force herself to dawdle along the path, to stop and literally smell the wild flowers rather than quickly head back to the village to see if there was anything she could do to help. She was ashamed of herself for having impure motives because now that she'd kissed Archer, all she wanted was to do it again and again. She wanted to sit and talk to him, *really* talk, to find out more about him, about his plans, about his dreams.

'Those kisses might not mean anything to him,' she rationalised as she finally headed back towards the village. Perhaps Archer was the type of man to only start a relationship with a woman he knew would be leaving soon. As Cora's contract expired in just under two weeks, she now fitted that profile. He would manage to have a bit of fun before she left and then he'd go back to being as free as a bird when she was safely back in Australia.

She frowned as she headed to the food hut, which was where she'd arranged to meet Melora. Somehow she couldn't picture Archer doing anything like that, but then again she really didn't know him all that well.

At the food hut she was delighted when Nee-Ty ran to her, his arms wide, the instant he saw her. Cora scooped the little boy up into her arms and hugged him close before he wriggled free of her hold and dragged her to where a few of the younger children were taking it in turns to stir a big bowl of freshly squeezed juice. The older children were the ones squeezing the fruit, which looked like pears but tasted more like pineapples.

Nee-Ty made her watch as he took a turn stirring the bowl and she dutifully oohed and ahhed and clapped in appreciation of his new skill before she and Melora took the kids to the craft hut for a few hours. During this time Cora managed to make enquiries about Archer's patient, Bunda.

'How is he?' she asked Sue, and felt guilty that she was using a patient update to garner information as to Archer's whereabouts.

'Archer's taken him back to Theatre. He thinks there's another rupture and without an X-ray the only way to be one hundred per cent sure is to open him up again.'

'Poor Bunda,' Cora returned, her concern for the patient quite genuine. She was going to ask Sue more questions but Nee-Ty once more demanded her attention and she was glad to give it to him. She had a lovely afternoon, doing craft, playing games, and she even managed to get a few hours' sleep while Melora looked after Nee-Ty.

'He can sleep in the green hut with the boys again while you're on night duty,' Melora suggested, but Cora shook her head.

'I have to get used to doing this. Being aware that I have a three-year-old to constantly think about.'

'It wouldn't be all that foreign to you, especially as you've helped raise your siblings.'

'That's true, and back home those thoughts are natural but here, in Tarparnii, I've never had to do that before.'

Melora chuckled. 'It'll become second nature before you know it.'

When evening time came, they all went to the food hut together and fed the children before Keith pulled out his guitar and several PMA staff as well as the villagers and visiting families gathered around the fire pit in the centre of the village. The smoke from the fire had a sweeter scent and was designed to repel insects as well as provide a low level of warmth.

With Nee-Ty seated in her lap, Cora rocked him to and fro as she joined in with singing one of her favourite lullabies. Songs were sung in English and Tarparnese and the atmosphere of total inclusion was paramount. It helped confirm to Cora that she was indeed doing the right thing with Nee-Ty.

'Hi.' At the sound of Archer's voice, she looked up and instantly smiled.

'How's Bunda?'

'Stable in Recovery.' He indicated the vacant seat beside her. 'May I?'

'Of course.' She was so happy he'd managed to finish in Theatre to join in with this wonderful community spirit. She was even happier that he'd sought her out. Neither of them spoke, enjoying the music for a while, Cora content just to be near him.

'How's Nee-Ty?' he asked when the song finished.

She looked down at the little boy in her arms,

whose eyelids were drooping. 'Almost asleep by the look of it. Oof. He's a deadweight when he sleeps.'

'Something else to get used to?' he asked.

'There's a lot to get used to. Melora's been helping me organise a temporary PMA visa so Nee-Ty can travel with me to Australia.'

'Things have moved fast.' He raised his eyebrows but due to the shadows being cast by the fire it was difficult for her to see whether he was happy about this turn of events or not.

'They have to. I'm due to leave in eleven days' time.'

'Hmm,' was his only reply. They sat in silence, listening to another few songs, before Cora's arms started aching.

'I think it's time to get Nee-Ty off to bed.' Feeling a little awkward, unsure about so many things where Archer was concerned, Cora shifted the sleeping boy in her arms so his head rested on her shoulder and stood.

'You really are a natural.'

'A natural?'

'A natural-born mother.' He nodded as though his words provided him with clarity.

'Thank you.' With a smile she turned and headed towards the huts, leaving Archer to sit at the fire, enjoying the music. What did it all mean, though? The man had kissed her like she'd never been kissed before, the tension between them so real and vibrant and addictive. Even just now she'd had a difficult time stopping herself from leaning over to kiss him before she'd left.

As she went through the motions of settling Nee-Ty and chatting quietly with Melora before reporting to the admin tent to sign in for her shift, thoughts of Archer remained as a constant at the back of her mind.

Throughout her shift, monitoring patients in both the intensive care tent and the recovery tent, Cora tried not to focus on the plethora of questions she wanted to ask him. She knew he'd been happier with the idea of Nee-Ty remaining in Tarparnii as part of Nahkala's village but now that she'd changed the programme, how did he feel? Did he want to be a part of Nee-Ty's life? Would he want to accept his role as guardian, too? If he did, what did that mean for her plans to have Nee-Ty in Australia with her?

More importantly, she wanted to know exactly

what that kiss had meant to him. Was she just some passing fancy or was it something more real? Because for her it was definitely the latter.

At around four-thirty in the morning, with the first greys of dawn starting to appear through the leaves in the trees, Cora did a round of her recovery patients before heading to the intensive care tent.

There she found the man from her thoughts standing by Bunda's bed, reading the nursing charts. Cora walked up to him and spoke softly. 'He's doing well this time, responding well to the antibiotics, and there's no sign of fever. And when we changed the wound site dressing, I noticed some very neat stitching. Nicely done, Dr Wild.'

The light-hearted use of his title, especially out here in the jungle where everyone was on a first-name basis, was enough to make his lips twitch with the beginnings of a smile. 'Thank you.' Archer stared at her for a moment before focusing himself and returning his attention to the duty at hand. He indicated the chart. 'We may even be able to decrease his pain relief.'

'That's a positive sign.'

Archer agreed, the two of them standing at the base of Bunda's makeshift bed, trying to think of something else to say. Archer had such a presence about him and one that she was becoming more and more drawn to with each passing second she spent with him. It didn't matter whether those moments were good or bad, only that she was able to get to know him better. It was so odd. No man had ever really captured her complete attention like this before and she wasn't at all sure how best to proceed.

'Nee-Ty settled all right?' he eventually said.

'Yes. He's been playing with Melora and Daniel's children, listening to them tell him all about Australia.' She smiled. 'I have no idea how much is actually sinking in, especially as a few days ago he'd never even been on a truck, so I think his concept of flying to another country is a little bit beyond him.'

'Has he mentioned Ni-Kaowa?'

Cora nodded, her tone mellowing. 'He asked me once where she was and when could he see her again.' She sighed, her heart heavy with sadness for the child. 'Grief takes time.'

'Yes.' Archer's answer was so emphatic she looked up at him with concern.

'Are you all right?'

'Cora.' He returned the chart to Bunda's bed then jerked his thumb towards the door. 'Are you free now? Can we go somewhere to…to talk?'

'Uh…everything's settled with my patients so I guess I could take a break.'

'Good.' He nodded and headed out of the tent. She followed him and found him at the central circle, the fire having died out quite a while before. It was still quite warm, especially with the sun beginning to wake. Archer grabbed two of the folding chairs and positioned them so they could see the entrance to both the recovery and intensive care tents—just in case they were needed.

'So you're really doing this?' He barely gave her time to draw breath before he dived right in.

'I'm really doing it,' she agreed, not bothering to play coy and pretend she had no clue what he was talking about. He liked that about her. Plain speaking. Good.

'What I'd really like to know is where you see me fitting into this equation.'

'Archer, I didn't agree to take Nee-Ty to lay guilt on you or put pressure on you or anything. You are more than welcome to be a positive influence in his life.' She smiled as she spoke, hoping her words didn't come across as dictatorial or confronting. 'Or a friend who we see a few times a year. Truly, Archer.' She leaned over and placed her hand on his. 'You shouldn't feel pressured.'

'But I do. That's just it and I have to confess, Cora, that in the past, whenever I've been pressured or backed into a corner, I've tended to come out fighting.'

Cora wasn't sure what to say or what to ask so she kept silent in the hope that after a moment Archer would continue to speak, to continue to open up. She'd meant what she'd said. She wasn't expecting anything from him.

'Always fighting.' He tilted his head back and looked up at the sky, his tone reflective. 'Although in the past the person I would usually be fighting when I felt this way was my father.' At the mention of his father Cora noticed the harshness in his tone. He'd already mentioned his father a few times and now, it seemed, he was ready to enlighten her a little bit more.

'You see, Cora, my father had the irritating habit of ordering, rather than asking. You never argued with him, you never quibbled or tried to voice your own opinion or point of view. You just did what was expected of you and that was that.'

He paused for a moment and looked across at Cora. 'When I was younger, all I wanted to do was to follow in his footsteps, to be a businessman like him. Of course, when I mentioned this to him at one point he scoffed, said I'd never make a good businessman.' He frowned, imitating his father's way of speaking. "You're weak. You care too much about people, about approval."' Archer paused and shook his head sadly. 'It was Daniel who suggested I do medicine *because* I cared about people. But all I could think was, Surely if I become a surgeon, my father will be proud of me. Right?'

Cora stayed silent, knowing he wasn't actually asking her the question.

He glanced down at his hands then back at her. 'Never. He was never proud of me, even though I tried to do everything he wanted.' Another pause. 'I even married the woman he told me to marry.'

Cora's eyebrows hit her hairline and a surge of annoyed anger filled her. 'You're married?' She stood from her chair and stared down at him. 'I can't believe you're married and yet...' she held out her hand towards the jungle behind them '...you *kissed* me.' She took a few steps away from him, shock and disbelief filling her every move.

'Cora—'

'Is that why you did your best to ignore the attraction between us?'

She paced up and down, wanting to walk off, to put some distance between the two of them, but the new morning light wasn't yet bright enough. Still, she couldn't believe the man before her, the one she hadn't been able to stop thinking about, was a married man!

'Cora.' He said her name more firmly, reaching out a hand to her. 'Will you just sit down and—?'

'And what? Let you...let you kiss me again?' She shook her head as though answering her own question. 'Not happening, buddy. I am not a home-wrecker.'

'Cora! You're not wrecking any home.'

That stopped her in mid-pace and she stared at him. 'What?'

'Will you just sit down?' He indicated the flimsy chair. 'Please?'

She did as he asked but leaned back as carefully as she could, still wanting to have a bit of distance between them. 'So are you married?'

'No.' He shook his head for emphasis. 'Not any more.'

'Oh. Divorced?'

'No. I'm a widower.'

The anger drained from Cora, to be replaced by sympathy. 'She died?'

'Yes.'

Poor Archer. With his father treating him like dirt, then losing his wife, it was little wonder he was closed off, preferring to hide behind military behaviour, stiff and starched, rather than being an open book like her.

'Even after my father's death,' he continued, clearly not wanting to say much more about his wife, 'his company advisers expected me to give up my career, my vocation, and return to England to take my rightful place as Chairman of the Board.'

'But clearly you haven't. You've stayed here, following your own path, and that's admirable.'

Archer slowly shook his head. 'What if this isn't the right path?'

'What do you mean?'

He opened his mouth to speak, to tell her that part of his motives, the main part in fact, for coming to work permanently in Tarparnii was so that he could try to forget his wife and the circumstances around her death. Helping others made him feel good and it assisted in combating the constant picture of Georgie being pulled from the water.

'Archer?' Her voice was filled with concern and he looked at her and shrugged.

'I don't like feeling pressured to do things, but what if sprinting from that pressure is the wrong thing to do?'

She thought on his words for a moment before choosing her words carefully, almost desperate to let him know that from her there was absolutely no pressure whatsoever. 'Archer, I'm not trying to make you do anything except what you want to do. Personally, when I accepted guardianship of Nee-Ty, I was only trying to follow my own heart. Remember that I've had a completely different upbringing from you, one surrounded with love and laughter, with far too many siblings, and I guess the thought of Nee-Ty being alone was too much for me to bear.' She sighed and looked directly into his eyes. 'Everybody needs somebody.'

Archer pondered her words for a moment before nodding, breaking his gaze from hers and focusing on his hands. 'My hands are the same size and shape as my father's,' he said after a moment. 'We both have long fingers and smallish palms. I was eight when I realised our bone structure was the same. At that time in my life, when I came home from boarding school for the holidays, I was desperate to garner my father's attention, to tell him of my scholastic aptitude, to impress him with my efforts to mix with the other boys, to become popular. These were the things I thought would make him proud of me because in his grown-up world *he* was popular and powerful and intelligent. People, businessmen, lords and viscounts and earls came to him for advice, and he was well respected within that structure of society and, oh, how I wanted to be like him, to make him proud of me.'

'I'm sure a lot of other eight-year-old boys feel the same way, wanting their father's approval.'

'I would wake early every morning at the crack of dawn in the hope that I would be able to see him, talk to him while he ate his breakfast. The first morning when I tried this tactic I walked boldly into the breakfast room and pulled out a chair and sat down, expecting him to lower his newspaper and be surprised that I was not only awake but clean and dressed and ready to start my day.'

Archer gazed unseeingly as colour started filtering into the grey of morning. 'He didn't. For a while I thought I'd been too quiet so I cleared my throat and tapped the spoon against my cereal bowl but still he didn't move, didn't look at me. He only turned the page in his newspaper and continued reading. That's when I noticed his hands. I held mine near his and compared them. One large, one small, and from that moment on I was desperate that my hands continued to grow like his, helping people, shaping the world with their cleverness.' He laughed without humour. 'Naivety at its best.'

'What happened next?' Cora asked, not wanting to deter him from his story, from this privileged insight into his childhood, because she had the oddest sensation that he rarely spoke about it. The brisk, military man had hidden himself behind rules and regulations because being soft and opening up, discussing his feelings, had been forbidden, first at home and then, no doubt, at the schools he'd been sent away to. Her heart ached for the Archer of the past as well as the Archer of the present.

'He finished reading his paper, lowered it, finished his cup of tea, wiped his mouth with a napkin, then stood and walked from the room with barely a glance in my direction. To all intents and purposes, I'd been invisible.'

'Oh, Archer. You must have been so crushed.'

'You would think that, right? Nope. The next morning I decided to repeat the exercise, to go down to breakfast even earlier, and be sitting at the breakfast table when he entered the room.'

'And did you?

'Yes. Every day for the rest of the two-week school vacation. I sat at that breakfast table so early that half the time the servants hadn't even set it.'

'And did he notice you? Talk to you?' Cora was hoping, willing the story to have a happy ending, but she could tell by the slight grimace on Archer's face that it wasn't to be the case.

'He never came. From that moment on and every other time I came home for vacation he would eat all his meals at his gentlemen's club.'

'Archer.' Cora reached over and took his hand in hers, lacing her fingers with his. 'How heartbreaking.'

'So I guess you could say that without firm role models in parenting, my mother suffering from depression and alcoholism and my father being non-existent in my life, that I feel…inadequate to recommend myself for such an occupation.'

'This is a very different situation. Nee-Ty adores you.'

'He does?'

'Yes. He calls you the carrying giant—I think

because you carried him on your back and your shoulders. He keeps asking where you are.'

'He does?' Archer repeated, clearly perplexed that the small boy actually found him interesting, but then he shook his head. 'He may find me OK to be around now but what about when he's eight or twelve or seventeen?'

Cora grinned. 'No parent has that answer, Archer.' Even the fact that Archer was discussing being a part of Nee-Ty's life was a step in the right direction.

'What if I'm my father?' The words were almost choked from his mouth, as though he'd been struggling whether or not to speak them out loud. 'I have his hands.'

She loosened her fingers from his and took one of his hands in both of hers, stroking first the back of his hand and then the palm. 'You may have the same hand bone structure as your father but you do amazing work with your hands, Archer. You save people's lives!' She angled her head towards the inside of the tent where several patients lay—alive—because of Archer's skills.

'Your father may have helped to shape society but you *save lives*. You've taken the rejection he served you as a child and you've used it for the good of others. You and Nee-Ty will not share the same hand bone structure but what you can pass on to him is the desire to help others, to do what you can to make a difference in this world. *Those* are qualities worthy of a parent and you have them in spades.'

'How can you be sure?'

'That's an easy question to answer. Because you saved my life.' She smiled at him and was delighted when he returned that smile, her body zinging to life once more. Did the man have any idea just how he affected her? How the need she'd ignored, the need for male companionship, for desire, for love—all of those things—became rampant whenever he was near? She may not have known him for long but she had the sense that she knew him better than most.

He'd taken a risk, opened up to her, shared his past hurts and his present reservations. How could she not feel drawn to him?

'Thank you, Dr Wilton.' He held her gaze while he raised her hand to his lips, brushing a soft kiss to her skin. 'Your words and encouragement have been…inspirational.'

Cora swallowed over the sudden dryness of her throat, her body angling naturally towards Archer's when he slid one hand slowly up her arm to rest on her shoulder.

'Cora. Seriously. I don't think you understand what it is you've done to me.' His words were soft, quiet and intimate. His breath mingled with hers as he leaned towards her, his gaze dipping to encompass her mouth as his hand slid to the back of her neck. 'I can't stop thinking about those kisses,' he whispered.

'Oh.' She trembled at his words, her breathing increasing, her lips parting with anticipatory delight.

'How is it that I've only known you for such a short time?'

'Does it matter?' she whispered.

'I don't think so.'

'Neither do I.'

He continued to move towards her, angling his head to the side as his gaze flicked between her eyes and her parted lips, wanting to taste the delights of the woman who was starting to change the way he saw himself.

'Is this a wise decision?' She couldn't help

but voice her reservations. If they were going to enter into a form of joint custody of a child, should they become romantically involved?

'Probably not,' he replied. 'But I can't resist the allure of your mouth any longer.'

Cora's lips turned upwards at his words, her heart melting with temporary happiness. 'Good answer.'

CHAPTER EIGHT

KISSING ARCHER WAS definitely far better in reality than in her dreams. Why was it that her mouth seemed to mesh with his in perfect synchronicity? How was it that she'd only known him for a few days and yet felt so right to be sitting here, kissing him? What was it that made him so irresistible she had been unable to fight her common sense any longer?

The slight touch of his other hand on her cheek as his fingers gently caressed her skin only intensified the way he was making her feel. He slid his hand around to the back of her neck, urging her closer, wanting to be nearer to her, and the knowledge that he was also affected by these incredible emotions delighted her. Whereas last time their kisses had been testing, rushed, almost forbidden, this time they were comfortable, slow and tender.

He tasted of power mixed with adrenaline,

blended with a healthy dose of sex appeal. As his tongue coaxed a slow and gentle response from her, almost questioning whether or not she wanted the kiss to continue, Cora sighed with longing and desire.

It had been a very long time since a man had been this attentive, kissing her in a way that let her know he wasn't just after a physical release. He was looking, searching for a pure emotional connection, which often seemed so elusive in the world. Out here, in the middle of the jungle, re-moved from a lot of societal pressures, the most complex things could seem so simple, so clear. She felt no pressure to please or to hide who she really was deep down inside. And as Archer's slow but thorough exploration of her mouth con-tinued, Cora breathed in his essence, the heady combination of spice, sweat and power.

There might be a huge question mark over whether kissing him was the right thing to do, especially given the strange turn of events that would govern their future. Regardless of what-ever involvement he decided on in Nee-Ty's life, the bond between *them* would continue. She knew enough of Archer to realise that he was a man who did the right thing, even when it seemed wrong. After all, hadn't he risked life and limb to rescue them?

She parted her lips, opening to him, and once again she was delighted at the way he didn't rush on ahead. He stayed with her, locked in the same moment, savouring the flavours of sweetness and sunshine that seemed to sum up the way he saw Cora. The woman was driving him insane. He couldn't believe how she'd managed to become so ingrained within him, as though she'd somehow found her way into his bloodstream and now there wasn't a moment that didn't pass without her being a part of it.

Sure, he'd only known her for a few days but somewhere in the far recesses of his mind he knew he'd been waiting a long time for Cora, for this most incredible woman to enter his life and to save him from the internal loneliness he hadn't spoken of to anyone. Even when she'd looked at him earlier—when he'd been telling her about his father—he'd seen that hint of sadness in her eyes, that sense that she understood the emotion behind his words—that she had somehow been able to truly *feel* that abandonment he'd experienced so long ago. How was it possible? How could a connection like this even exist? How was it possible that in kissing her he felt as though he'd finally found the one place in the world where he truly belonged?

That thought alone was what drew him away from the gloriousness of her mouth. He still cupped her face in his hands as he looked at her, swallowing over the need to continue his exploration as well as ignoring the wild thrumming of his heart. He watched as her heavy eyelids opened, just a fraction, but enough to meet his gaze.

Archer caught his breath. 'You are so beautiful,' he murmured, his words instantly rewarded with a small, shy smile, which only seemed to add more credence to his statement. 'Do you know that?' He eased back slightly and brushed his fingers through her short, dark hair, loving the feel of the silky strands against his rough skin.

'You can tell me as much as you like,' she countered. 'I'd never tire of hearing it.'

Now it was his turn to smile and as he leaned forward, unable to resist the urge to brush another kiss to her gorgeous, upturned mouth, Archer felt himself begin to overbalance. His eyes widened with the realisation that he was sitting in the flimsiest of folding chairs and combined with the angle at which he was leaning, was it any wonder the apparatus was collapsing beneath him?

'Wh-whoa!' He let go of her and tried to use his arms to steady himself. Even Cora reached out, her attempts thwarted by the bubble of laughter that burst forth from her lips. In the next instant he found himself face down on the ground, the chair in a mangled mess beneath his body. Cora's loud giggles did nothing for his self-esteem as he twisted himself around to lie on his back, pulling the now-deceased chair from beneath him.

'Oh, you think this is funny, do you?' he teased. Then, without warning, he reached for her hand and tugged her sideways, causing her own chair to overbalance and for her to land neatly in his arms. She was half lying on his torso, her legs on the ground, but his big, strong arms were securely around her, enveloping her, drawing her close.

'You fit perfectly in my arms, Dr Wilton,' he murmured, his gaze flicking between her half-closed eyes and her parted lips. 'I knew that from the first night we spent together.'

Cora lifted her head to look at him more clearly. 'The first night?'

He raised one eyebrow. 'You don't remember?'

'I remember sleeping...in comfort.' She said the last two words as though remembering something from a dream, a hint of confusion about her words.

'And that comfort would have been my arms wrapped securely around you, stopping your body from shivering and keeping you warm. Body heat.' He tenderly brushed her hair back from her face and tucked it behind her ear, much as he'd done the first instant he'd looked into her eyes. 'It's the best way to combat the effects of hypothermia.'

Cora's smile was slow and sensual as she shifted closer to him. 'What a hardship that must have been for you.'

'Oh, it was, but I do whatever it is that I need to do in order to get the job done and sometimes the things I have to do…well, let's just say this job does come with some pretty nice perks.'

Cora traced a small scar on the corner of his chin, idly wondering how he'd got it, as she spoke. 'And it's clear that you're very good at your job, Dr Wild, because, come morning, I was no longer cold. In fact…' She brought her mouth even closer to his own, her body nicely warmed from the heat they were producing, her senses completely drugged with the essence of him, her need for another fix intensifying. 'I woke up feeling absolutely wonderful.' She rubbed her finger to his lips, first the lower and then the upper. She'd never been this forward, this playful with a man…only with Archer.

'Yeah?' He captured her finger with his lips, drawing the tip into his mouth, causing her to gasp with delight.

'Ye-yeah,' she stammered. 'I had a dr-dream.' She closed her eyes as the sensations of pleasure and need and longing broke over her once more.

'Mmm-hmm?'

'Th-that you were holding me, keeping me… er…safe.' Didn't he realise it was incredibly difficult to concentrate, to form normal, ordinary, everyday sentences when he was setting her body alight with his sensual antics?

'Mmm?' He brought his hand to the back of her head, urging her mouth closer to his, and a moment later the kisses he'd been bestowing on her finger stopped as his lips met hers once again, both of them sighing into the sensation that was quickly becoming highly addictive.

This time there was no hesitation, only need. Cora opened her mouth willingly to his. Archer's hunger—barely controlled—was clearly apparent. Where his first initial kisses had been teasing, testing, tantalising, he now let her know just how she was affecting him.

'Perfect,' he whispered, as he intensified the pressure, clearly delighted when Cora matched his need. This was Archer, the man who had saved her life, and while there was a level of gratitude in her response there was also a lot of desire, of need, of pure sensual attraction, such as she'd never felt before.

'We should stop,' Archer said a few minutes later, his breathing ragged against hers. He accepted the three kisses she placed on his lips. 'Cora,' he whispered, and brushed her hair from her face. 'We really...' Another kiss. 'Need to stop.' Another kiss, then, 'We're a little...er... exposed.'

It was only then that Cora's senses began to shift, to return to normal. He was absolutely right. She'd completely forgotten they were practically lying as close as they could get, across from the recovery and intensive care tents, their flimsy chairs scattered haphazardly around them.

A giggle of incredulity bubbled forth and she pressed a hand to his chest to help right herself, the clamping the other across her mouth. As she sat up, so did Archer, and when they looked at each other, their mirth continued to erupt. Birds were chirping in the trees, daylight was filtering around them, lighting the area with the newness of the morning. Soon the village centre where they were right now would become a hive of activity.

'Oops.' She looked cautiously around them but, thankfully, couldn't see anyone. That, of course, didn't mean there wasn't anyone about.

'You do that to me,' Archer said, as he stole a quick kiss from her lips before clambering to his feet. He held out a hand to help her up before righting their chairs. 'You make me forget.'

'Is that a good thing?' she asked, pulling down on her shirt and tucking it into her trousers, unsure when she had become so dishevelled.

Her answer was a warm, deep chuckle from Archer. Next he took her hand in his and gave a gentlemanly bow before pressing a quick kiss to her knuckles. 'I'll let you get back to work,' he stated.

'Thanks.' She smiled at him but didn't let go of his hand. 'Are you going to try and get some rest?'

'I'm not all that tired right now.'

'Or you could spend some time with Nee-Ty,' she suggested, but instantly wished she hadn't as he let go of her hand, his expression turning from one of joviality to perplexed concern. She sighed, wishing she hadn't said anything, preferring to see happiness reflected in his eyes rather than anything else.

'Yes.'

'Everything will work itself out, Archer,' she offered, trying to encourage him. 'Just…enjoy being with him because at the end of the day that's what it really is all about.'

He nodded once, his face still etched with uncertainty. 'I hope the rest of your shift is uneventful,' he stated, taking a few steps away from her.

'Me, too.' She turned to go into the tent but couldn't resist a glance back at him. She watched him walk towards where Daniel and Melora were staying, his back straight, arms swinging by his sides with military precision. Stiff and starched. It made her think of what he'd told her, of how he'd been raised by either nannies or boarding-school rules and regulations. How much love had Archer experienced during his life? It certainly sounded as though familial love had been severely lacking. The knowledge saddened her heart. If only Archer could have experienced a fraction of the parental and sibling love she had delighted in for her entire life, he might see that adopting Nee-Ty was the right decision.

As Cora entered the tent, ignoring the very interested glances from the nurse, who had no doubt witnessed the passionate kisses, she decided that perhaps instead of telling Archer everything would work out fine with Nee-Ty she should show him. If he could see her with her crazy, loud and loving family, he'd see how this arrangement suited everyone but most of all Nee-Ty.

'Yes.' She nodded as she crossed to her patient's side to check his vitals. 'I'll invite Archer home for Christmas.'

Cora finished her shift and went in search of Nee-Ty, only to be told by Melora that Daniel and Archer had taken the children, including Nee-Ty, for a walk to the waterhole.

'Did you say something to Archer about trying to bond with Nee-Ty?' her friend asked her.

'Uh…' Cora angled her head to the side, trying to remember exactly what she'd said, because when she thought of Archer all that came into her head was the way he made her feel when he held her close, when he gazed into her eyes, when he pressed his lips to hers. She sighed dreamily then gave her head a little shake. 'I think I mentioned something like that. Why?'

'It's just that I've never seen him so…soft before.' Melora frowned. 'I think that's the right word. Usually, even around our children—or any children, for that matter—he's all brisk and a bit standoffish, but not this morning. He was sitting on the ground, making dirt roads with a stick so the boys had somewhere to drive their little rock cars. He's never done anything like that before.' She held up her hands. 'Not that I'm criticising him. It's not that Archer doesn't like children, it's just that, until this morning, he didn't seem to know how to relate to them.'

'Huh.' Cora nodded and smiled. 'Well, it's a start and it's great that he's trying.' Her heart warmed at the thought of him playing in the dirt. She smothered a yawn and quickly apologised, telling her friend she was going to get some sleep. 'And hopefully,' she murmured to herself as she settled down on a spare mat in purple hut, 'the boys will be back when I wake up.' She smiled at the thought and chuckled as she closed her eyes. 'The boys. My boys,' she sighed, and drifted off to sleep.

'You seem a little agitated today,' Daniel remarked, as he and Archer walked back towards the village, the children running on ahead, drying out from their swim in the beautiful sunshine.

'I'm not agitated.' There was no animosity in his words, just a statement of fact.

'Pensive, then.' Daniel tried again.

Archer looked at his friend and nodded. 'There is much to be pensive about.'

'Nee-Ty?'

'Yes.'

'What are you going to do?'

'I'm not sure.'

'Weighing up all the pros and cons. I get that. I mean…' Daniel spread his hands wide '…I think it's great that you're spending time with him today. That little boy has no one.'

'No one except Cora,' Archer proffered.

Daniel agreed. 'She's an amazing person. Not many women would take on the responsibility of an orphaned child the way she has, especially one from a completely different culture. It's as though she made the decision and that was that. In her mind, Nee-Ty is her son. She loves him unconditionally.'

It took a lot of heart to do such a thing and

Archer had already realised that Cora had such a capacity for other people, for listening to them, for supporting them, for loving them. Somehow she had come to mean a great deal to him in a very short space of time and earlier that morning, when he'd held her close, her mouth responding to his, he had felt…happy. Cora had made him feel happy for the first time in far too long. 'But how?'

'How what?' Daniel asked, and it was only then that Archer realised he'd spoken out loud. He shook his head, but Daniel was an astute friend, who instantly grinned. 'You're thinking about Cora.'

Archer let go of his restraint and spread his arms wide. 'What am I supposed to do about her?'

'What do you want to do?' Daniel's grin was almost wolfish and Archer shook his head.

'We're not teenagers any more. I just can't…I don't know…understand how she's become so constant in my thoughts in such a short time.'

'Why do you need to understand it?' At Archer's glare, Daniel quickly continued. 'I know that's your thing. You have an analytical mind and if things make logical sense, then you're fine with it. It was how you approached your schoolwork, your relationship with your father and even your marriage to Georgie.'

'Hey. I loved Georgie.'

'I'm not saying you didn't but in the beginning, what was it about Georgie that you fell in love with? Was it the way she was constantly plaguing your thoughts, the way she acted towards others, the way she looked? What was it?'

Archer stopped walking and thought for a moment, remembering the smile on Georgie's face whenever he'd return home for his annual vacation. While most of his other vacations had been spent with Daniel, every year he was required to spend at least one vacation at home. He had no idea why his father had insisted on that stipulation and at the time he hadn't questioned it, but years later he'd wondered if it had had anything to do with the eventual relationship he'd fallen into with Georgie.

They'd always spent time together during those vacations, horse-riding, hiking, rock-climbing— well, he'd rock-climb and she'd cheer him on. They'd become friends because Georgie had been a good listener and she'd been sweet and pretty, but she hadn't been a constant feature in his thoughts, not the way Cora was right now.

'Georgie was…sweet,' he eventually confessed.

'Yes, she was.' Daniel's tone was quiet, respectful. 'And because of her sweetness, she wouldn't have wanted you to shut yourself off from the rest of the world. She'd want you to find happiness again.'

'Are you suggesting I can find that happiness with Cora?'

'Perhaps. Maybe being a part of Nee-Ty's life, whether here or in Australia, might be the key to that happiness.' Daniel stopped walking and placed a hand on his friend's shoulder. 'Try not to overthink things. I know that's difficult because that's just who you are, but instead of analysing things why not go with your gut instinct?'

'Hmm.' Archer frowned, considering his friend's words. Daniel laughed and continued walking.

'What's your instinct telling you to do regarding Cora? Don't think, just say the first thing that comes to mind.'

Archer raised an eyebrow at that and Daniel chuckled. 'OK, the second thing.'

'To spend some more time with her. Alone. Away from Nee-Ty, away from the village.'

'Then do that. Take her hiking or climbing. She's the adventurous type so you at least have that in common.'

'Go with my gut,' he remarked, as the concept started to appeal to him more and more. 'OK. I'll ask Cora out on a date.'

'Excellent. We'll look after Nee-Ty for the two of you.'

'It'll have to be in a few days' time, once all the extra clinics we're having settle down.'

'Of course, and in the meantime can I just suggest that you continue to spend more time with that cute little boy? He really responds well to you.'

'That's what Cora said.'

'She's a smart woman…and she seems to like you a lot, too.' They'd reached the edge of the village and Daniel patted his friend on the back. 'Go for it, mate. You deserve happiness.'

Archer watched as Daniel jogged over to

where Melora was sitting and pressed a kiss to his wife's lips. Did he deserve happiness? He still wasn't convinced.

CHAPTER NINE

FOR THE NEXT few days Cora felt as though she was walking on pillows of feathers on air. The sun was always shining and even though they were busy with clinics and patients still arriving in the village almost a week since the cyclone had hit, many having walked a very long way, the urgency of the situation had started to settle down.

The villagers from Nee-Ty's village had started returning to begin rebuilding their homes. None of them said goodbye to the little boy, not giving him another thought now that he was no longer their problem. And although Cora was annoyed by their behaviour, it also helped to solidify in her heart that she'd made the right decision.

Her love for the child grew daily and for the past few nights, when she hadn't been on night shift, he'd slept beside her in the purple hut, snuggling close as they had been that night the cyclone had hit. The difference in the little boy was quite amazing. He now had people who cared about him, friends who liked to play with him. He no longer needed to sit on the step of a hut and wait to be told what to do as, along with all the other children in the village, he now had his daily list of chores. He'd pick berries, gather kindling and do other small jobs.

He talked of 'Australia' with glee, listening intently as Melora's children told him about their home and their life in the other country. Although Cora knew he couldn't possibly comprehend everything that would soon be happening to him, she only hoped the bond she was forming with him was enough to help him through the transition.

Where Archer was concerned, Cora hadn't yet found the right moment to ask him whether he'd like to accompany herself and Nee-Ty back to Australia for Christmas. Having him by her side throughout the journey would certainly help Nee-Ty, especially as Archer spoke the same dialect as the little boy. She was still getting the odd word wrong.

The two of them had been managing to spend

a bit more time together, mainly in the evenings when they'd sit and chat with some of the other PMA staff or join in with the village community activities. Several times Nee-Ty had chosen to sit in Archer's lap and Cora had been pleased with the way Archer was slowly becoming more natural around the child, especially holding him close when Nee-Ty fell asleep.

Last night, though, when Archer had carried Nee-Ty back to the purple hut, the little boy had cried when Archer had put him on the sleeping mat, clinging to Archer and declaring he didn't want him to leave.

'Why don't you stay?' Cora had asked, as she'd taken off her boots and adjusted the sleeping mats. There were still several people who called the purple hut their home so one more wouldn't matter.

'Are you sure?' he'd asked, Nee-Ty's arms still around his neck.

'It'll be easier and he'll settle sooner,' she remarked, yawning a little. Every night since Archer had kissed her he'd walked her to her hut and spent a few minutes kissing her good-night, before returning to his own. The perfect gentleman.

As he relented and lay down next to Nee-Ty, Cora on the opposite side of the boy, Archer stared over the child's head, directly into her eyes. For the moment they were alone in the hut but it wouldn't be long before other PMA staff turned in for the night.

'He's holding on so tight,' Archer remarked, and Cora couldn't help by smile.

'It's understandable. You're probably the first male he can ever remember taking an interest in him. Why wouldn't he want to hold on to you?'

Archer considered her words for a moment before nodding. 'I hadn't thought of it like that.'

'Does that make you feel even more pressure to become a part of his life?'

Archer's smile was natural at her words and Cora instantly responded to it with a sigh and a smile of her own. 'I think I'm already a part of his life.'

'I think you're right.' She bit her lip, her thoughts racing ahead.

'Just say it, Cora.'

'Pardon?'

'You're biting your lip. It either means you're trying to figure out how to say something or you're concerned.'

'Or both.'

'Either way—just say it.' Because the sight of her biting her lips was so incredibly appealing it was difficult for him not to lean across and claim her lips with his own. The kisses they'd shared over the past two days had become rather addictive and he'd found himself wanting to kiss her more and more throughout the day but had disciplined himself to wait for evening. Discipline. It had been one of the prominent ruling forces in his life and it was still something he relied on, especially where his attraction to Cora was concerned.

'OK.' She paused, then took another breath before saying softly, 'I was wondering if you'd like to accompany Nee-Ty and myself back to Australia next week. That way we can both be there for his first Christmas.'

'But you'll be with your family.' Even the thought of being in a room with all of Cora's siblings started to fill him with anxiety. It wasn't that he didn't like crowds; he was fine in a crowd because in a crowd no one knew who you were, but in a family, a loving, close-knit family, people…expected things of you, expected you to join in, to do your part, to talk about personal things.

'I know. They'd all love to meet you.'

His eyes widened. 'All of them?' He gulped and had to stop himself from shaking his head. How many siblings did she have? Five? Plus, she'd mentioned that her sister Stacey was married so that added an extra person to the mix.

Cora chuckled. 'Of course.' She reached out and placed a hand on his shoulder, her eyes bright with happiness. 'They might be a bit much to take in at the beginning but you'll adjust quickly and we don't have to stay with them at home if you don't want to.'

Her whole family under the one roof? How big was the house? It wasn't that he didn't like close-knit communities. Here, in Tarparnii, he loved the village lifestyle, where everyone had a job to do and pitched in to help run the village, but was it like that in Cora's family? Would he be able to just go for a walk when things got too much? He wasn't used to living in the Western world, wasn't used to the rules of society. They boxed him in, made him feel trapped…Cora was making him feel trapped just by asking him to spend Christmas with her.

How on earth was he supposed to cope when he came face to face with all those siblings? All of them. With their high expectations, watching him, testing him, warning him against hurting their sister. He'd rather battle another cyclone or wrestle a wild animal. He was trained for situations like that. He wasn't trained for dealing with families.

However, he had to remind himself that she wasn't asking him to come just because she wanted him there for Christmas. She wanted him to come to help support Nee-Ty's transition from Tarparnii to Australia. He'd be helping and he did like to help others where possible. She'd told him a few days ago that, as far as she was concerned, he could be involved in Nee-Ty's life as much or as little as he wanted. Therefore the question became, what exactly did he want?

'I think,' he remarked after a moment, knowing he would probably regret his next words, 'accompanying you to Australia might be a good idea. That way, as you've said, I can assist you with Nee-Ty as he transitions into a foreign environment.' He was doing this for Nee-Ty. He had to keep reminding himself of that.

She caressed his cheek and the smile in her eyes turned to one of sad happiness. 'Such a logical thinker. That's not an insult,' she quickly added. 'It just makes me sad for the loveless upbringing you had to endure.'

He nodded, understanding what she was saying as well as enjoying the touch of her hand against his cheek. He reached up and took her hand in his, kissing the knuckles and then loosening Nee-Ty's grip around his neck, the child now sound asleep. 'It's because of my loveless childhood that I cannot allow the same thing to happen to Nee-Ty. He deserves to be loved, as you've said.'

He shifted onto his elbow before leaning over the boy and brushing his lips to Cora's. 'Thank you for showing me that, for encouraging me to become a part of his life. It's good for me, just as it's good for him.' He kissed her a few more times, breathing in her scent and allowing it to relax his usually taut muscles.

Cora sighed and he took that as a sign to deepen the kiss. 'You are exquisite,' he murmured against her mouth a while later. 'I don't know what it is you've done to me, Cora, but... everything's changing.'

'I hope you think it's changing for the better,' she said, feeling completely relaxed, her eyes beginning to close.

'I do,' he returned, and kissed her once more before settling down, Nee-Ty still sleeping soundly between them.

'Archer?' Her words were sleepy.

'Yes?'

'Will you help me make an internet call tomorrow? I need to let my sister know to set two more places at the Christmas table.'

He smiled at her sleep, slurred words. 'Of course.'

'Thank you,' she replied, and within another moment her breathing was that of a woman who had drifted off into a contented sleep. He stared up at the thatched roof of the hut, trying not to second-guess himself. Making Cora smile, seeing her eyes light with laughter was starting to become as addictive as her kisses, and he found himself trying to think of little ways in which he could achieve that goal. Going to Australia with her made sense—logical sense—but the thought of meeting Cora's entire family, especially when he knew how close she was to them and how important their opinions were to her, filled him with increasing doubts.

He closed his eyes, pushing the thoughts aside for now. Tomorrow they needed to make an internet call and he needed to reserve all his strength for that.

'So you like doing the adventure thing?' he called up to her, as she dangled from a cliff face by one hand. She reached around her body and dipped her hand into a little bag at her waist, which held some chalk so she could get a firm grip on the corner of the next boulder. Both of them were tethered to abseiling ropes, which were tied off below.

'It makes me feel alive,' she yelled back, after she'd safely made it to her next handhold. She found a small ledge and slipped her foot into it to give herself more stability while she waited for him to join her. 'Come on, slowpoke,' she taunted, and was rewarded with a rich, deep chuckle.

While she waited for him, she gazed out over her shoulder at the incredible scenery spread before her. Although they were further around the island from where the cyclone had made its initial impact, there were still several areas where trees had been flattened and uprooted. Yet she could see people in the distance, working together as a team to rectify the situation.

That was another reason why she liked coming to Tarparnii. The sense of camaraderie, of community was so strong and so ingrained that at times she wished the Western world could employ some of the same tactics in order for everyone to get along better. She guessed that being a triplet meant she was used to working as part of a team so it came very naturally to her.

'And what,' Archer said as he pulled himself up to her level, 'may I ask, are you staring at?'

Cora's answer was to grin as she turned her attention to him. 'I'm staring at this beautiful country and realising that I'm going to enjoy not needing to find an excuse to come back for visits. This is Nee-Ty's home, his heritage, and I want to learn as much about it as I possibly can.'

Archer nodded. 'He was upset that he couldn't come climbing with us but at least he's happy playing with Melora's children.'

'He said good morning to me in English.' Cora's smile was wide and bright and she shook her head with delight. 'He's quite amazing.'

'He is, and no doubt it won't be too many years before he *is* big enough to come rock-climbing with us.'

'And he'll probably beat us both to the top,' she added, her heart and words filled with love for the little boy.

'Speaking of which, up you go, Dr Wilton. You have an important event to get to.'

Cora chuckled but didn't argue. Instead, she focused her attention on finding the next hand- and foothold before levering herself up. As she climbed, she couldn't stop her heart from delighting in hearing Archer use the word *us*.

She still had a thousand questions but for once she wasn't madly searching for answers. Where previously in her life she'd had to find ways to stop herself from thinking about a childless future, she now had different concerns to fill her mind. Adopting Nee-Ty under Australian law would take some time, but what sort of arrangements did Archer want?

Would he return to Tarparnii after Christmas? Would he take Nee-Ty with him? How were they going to maintain contact? What sort of schedule did Archer have in mind? What were his thoughts about Nee-Ty's future? These were the same questions that had churned in her mind on constant repeat.

Added to all of those questions were the ones she had regarding her relationship with Archer. What did all the kissing and cuddling mean to him? Was he looking for another permanent relationship? Was he ever going to tell her more about his wife? About what had happened? Was she nothing more than a pleasant distraction for him? She knew he'd been raised to keep his emotions under control but it made it incredibly difficult for her to try and gauge his mood.

Was he falling for her, just as she was falling for him? She wasn't the type of woman to give her heart easily, especially when, in the past, she'd been dumped because she couldn't have children. Although Nee-Ty had filled that gap in her life, *should* anything more permanent transpire between herself and Archer, did he want more children?

She sighed with frustration and shook her head, clearing her thoughts. Hanging in the middle of a cliff by her fingertips was probably not the best location to have a mental breakdown. Focusing on the task at hand, Cora resumed her climb.

When she finally reached the top she felt exhilarated. The adrenaline had been useful to propel her up the cliff but now that she'd accomplished it, she felt fantastic. She unclipped her rope and moved to stand away from the edge. 'Beautiful!' she called, breathing in the lovely fresh air.

'Would you look at that view!' She spoke the words to Archer as his powerful arms and strong legs flexed as he levered himself up over the lip and onto the plateau.

He stood before her and spread his warms wide. 'Do you mean *this* view?' he asked, and surprised her with a wink.

Cora's smile was instant, loving this slightly less serious side to Archer. 'No.' She laughed and forced herself to look away from his gorgeousness. '*That* view.' She indicated the spectacular scenery before them and Archer straightened, coming to her side and placing his arm firmly around her shoulders. She leaned into him.

'Oh. *That* view. Yes. It *is* spectacular.' He took a moment to absorb the world around them before his gaze settled on her. 'And this view, too.' He looked down into her upturned face. 'This view is quite spectacular as well.'

With that, he lowered his head and claimed her lips, just as he'd done so many times before. Cora wondered whether she'd ever get used to the sensations that zinged to life, exciting her body into a trembling mass of desire and want. It wasn't just the physical contact she loved but the way Archer seemed to genuinely care about her, that he liked spending time in her company just talking, that he respected her. For a man who'd closed himself off, who rarely allowed others to see into his inner soul, he was being incredibly generous with her and she wanted him to know she appreciated it.

'Thank you for coming climbing with me,' he murmured against her lips.

'Are you kidding? How else am I supposed to make my internet call?' She winked back at him and he brushed one more kiss across her lips before releasing her.

He drank in the view. 'This is one of my favourite cliffs to climb.'

'You have more favourites?' she asked, as she held out her hand for the satchel, which was securely clipped to his waist. Archer immediately undid it and handed it to her. 'What are the others?'

'There's one in New Zealand, one in America and…' he thought for a moment '…one in Switzerland.'

Her eyes widened as she looked up from where she was setting up her satellite computer. 'The Matterhorn?' His answer was to grin. 'Wow. I've only ever ridden the ride at the amusement parks.'

Archer chuckled at her answer, watching as she turned the computer on, trying to control his rising trepidation at 'meeting' her siblings. It was clear to him, however, that Cora really did love the adventuring, and while she tried to get the chat working, she told him about some of her other rock-climbing exploits. He was pleased to discover they'd actually climbed at some of the same places and he felt a pang of regret that they hadn't done it together.

'What about white-water rafting?' As he spoke the words his mouth dried up and he quickly unclipped his water bottle and took a swig. Did she like it? Had she tried it? Did she understand the dangers inherent to the sport? Would she go just because someone asked her to?

'I've tried it. Twice, in fact. The first time was on a very tame—if you could call it that—river in Perth, but when I went to New Zealand, wow, what a ride. It was super-scary.'

'Would you go again?'

'Probably not.'

'What if I asked you to go?' It was a test. A big test.

Cora glanced up at him, a curious look in her eyes. Had she heard the undercurrent of concern in his words? Could she guess what was behind his questions? Had Daniel or Melora already told Cora about how Georgie had died?

'Um…I'd probably go. I mean, I trust you, so I'm sure you would have checked things out to make sure everything was safe.' She smiled warmly at him.

'But accidents can happen.' There was an urgency to his tone and Cora gave him a quizzical look. 'People do die when they do extreme, adventurous things.'

She nodded. 'I know, but there's risk in everything. In crossing the street, driving in a car, undergoing surgery. It's why we check, double-check and triple-check.' She knocked on the helmet she wore before taking it off and fluffing up her hair. 'Speaking of which, once I reset this connection for the third time, we should be able to get through…and… Aha, there's the picture!'

Cora turned her attention to the computer, her smile wide and bright and filled with pure happiness at seeing her siblings on the screen. 'Hi.' She blew kisses and waved. The speaker allowed him to hear the conversation clearly and when one of her sisters asked where she was calling from this time, Cora had no compunction in picking up the computer and slowly turning it around so the rest of her family could enjoy the view, too. Unfortunately, it also meant that he was captured as part of the picture.

'Ooh. Ooh. Go back.'

'To which part?' Cora asked, glancing up at Archer, her eyes dancing with delight.

'To the gorgeous man standing near you, you idiot.'

Cora laughed. 'Molly. Stop. You'll scare him.'

'Of course I will. It's my right as a sibling. Get him in front of this computer so we can all meet him.'

Cora beckoned him over but Archer shook his head. He'd rather abseil down this cliff face head first or climb the Matterhorn again or weather another close call with a cyclone than meet Cora's family. People were judgmental, critical and sometimes downright cruel.

'It's OK.' Her words were full of encouragement as she held out her hand to him. 'They don't bite.'

'But Cora might if you ask her nicely,' Molly returned, and the rest of Cora's siblings hooted with laughter before Stacey, her other sister, told Molly to behave and to stop scaring poor Archer.

They knew his name? They knew about him?

Of course he'd known that Cora had been in constant phone contact with her siblings but he hadn't realised she'd talked about him.

Cora still sat there, with her hand outstretched towards him. He knew if he said firmly that he didn't want to join in she would respect his decision, but she would be disappointed. He knew her well enough to know that for sure and the thought of disappointing her, of seeing sadness creep into her beautiful, hypnotic eyes, caused his gut to knot with guilt. He couldn't disappoint her and the realisation surprised him. It meant that Cora really had worked her way through his defences, whether he'd willing allowed her access or not. She started to lower her arm and he saw her happiness begin to change to sadness. That's when he forced himself to move towards her.

His reward was her magnificent smile, aimed solely at him. It warmed his heart, making it beat faster, and as he touched her hand, linking his fingers with hers, he felt as though she was passing her inner strength to him. She leaned forward so her siblings couldn't see them for a moment and whispered in his ear,

'You protected me throughout the cyclone. Let me protect you throughout the whole "meeting the family" ordeal.'

'You'll be my superhero?' he asked, his words barely audible as his gaze settled on her lips.

'Absolutely.' With that, she kissed him and all his tensions, all his doubts and concerns seemed to melt away…at least for now. He shifted around so he was facing the computer screen and sat down next to Cora.

'Hello. I'm Archer,' he said, and was treated to a cacophony of voices calling excited hellos and Molly's loud tones declaring he had a dishy, delightful accent. The craziness of her siblings made him laugh and Cora leaned into him, sighing with happiness that he was willing to do this for her, willing to meet her family, willing to open himself up. She'd seen that internal struggle he'd fought, seen it reflected in his eyes, but he'd broken through the barriers his father's rejection had put in place. He'd risked the possibility of getting hurt and he'd risked it for her.

Her heart swelled with love for him. Love? The instant the word popped into her mind the smile dropped from her face. She glared directly at the screen, into the eyes of Stacey and Molly, knowing they'd both clearly witnessed her own self-realisation.

For one split second her sisters stared back at her. Not one of the three spoke but that didn't stop the communication from happening. These were the two people who knew her better than she knew herself and Cora instinctively knew they were all on the same page. Molly and Stacey had just witnessed their sister realising she was in love with the man beside her.

'Oh, yay!' Molly was the first to break the silence and started clapping her hands. Stacey instantly told her to shush but tilted her head and stared at Cora.

'It's quite a ride,' Stacey murmured.

'What? What ride?' Archer asked, his tone snapping Cora out of her triplet bond.

'Er…um…' Thankfully, Stacey took the need for her to explain anything as she asked Archer how his patients were progressing. A nice, safe topic that was guaranteed to make Archer feel less of a sideshow alley attraction and more like an accepted member of her family.

'Well, hopefully that wasn't too painful,' Cora

remarked a while later, as she packed up the computer.

'Actually, it wasn't.'

She grinned. 'You sound surprised.'

'Well, I've never met a family en masse via satellite before.'

Cora hugged the computer to her chest and smiled dreamily. 'They are pretty special to me.'

'You miss them.' It was a statement and she nodded. 'Then why do you travel? Seek adventure? Come here?'

'So I can help others. I love my family more because they don't restrict me. They support me.'

'It's a foreign world you live in,' he remarked, as he took the computer from her and placed it back into the secure satchel, before pulling her into his arms. 'But meeting them has helped me understand you a bit better.'

'It has?' Cora settled herself into his arms, slipping hers around his waist as she lifted her face, ready for the kisses she knew would come. They were standing on top of the world, or at least it felt like it. The isolation up here was lovely, just the two of them, especially after the noisiness of her family, but it wasn't how she wanted to live the rest of her life. She couldn't remain isolated and yet that was the way Archer had lived his life for far too long.

She loved him. She loved this man. The more the word 'love' floated around in her mind, the more she recognised it for the truth that it was. She'd fallen in love with a man who could possibly be an emotional nomad, happy to try new things, to seek adventure, a thrill, a rush. as well as helping others in their time of need. He was her superhero, the man who had rescued her, but that wasn't why she loved him.

She loved him because he gave and gave and gave without ever asking for anything in return. How would he react if she offered him her love? Would he reject it? She closed her eyes for a moment, knowing this wasn't the moment to test the waters. Her own emotions were so new, so fresh, so uncharted but neither was she going to lie to herself and pretend they didn't exist. That would get her nowhere.

'You and Stacey and Molly. I don't know, it just seems…right, seeing the three of you like that, especially during that strange moment where you all just stared at each other.' His tone was quizzical, as were his raised eyebrows. 'What was that about?'

Cora forced a laugh and shrugged one shoulder. 'Just…triplet stuff.'

'What? Like sensing each other?'

'I guess.'

He looked over her, releasing her from his inquisitive gaze. 'I've read papers on the way twins and triplets can communicate with each other in such a way. It's not telepathy or anything like that, just an…' He searched for the word.

'Essence?' She closed her eyes and nodded. 'I know. It can be rather…' She thought of the way both Stacey and Molly had stared at her, had realised at the same moment that Cora had fallen in love with the man who'd had his arms around her. 'Unnerving.'

'Really? You're unnerved?'

'Not now.' She shifted a little closer to him, wanting to change the subject because the last thing she wanted to do was to lie to him about exactly what that 'essence' had contained. 'Now all I can think about is being on top of the world, with you.'

'Alone.'

'Together.' She stood on tiptoe, eager to have his lips pressed against hers. He kissed her in a way that made her feel as though she was floating on air. She was in love with Archer Wild. She should feel happy, elated, delighted, but instead there was a niggling worry at the back of her mind that by falling in love with him she'd just created even more problems for herself…because she wasn't sure he could ever love her back.

CHAPTER TEN

As THE TIME neared for Cora to leave Tarparnii, her second contract with PMA coming to
an end, Nee-Ty started to become very clingy.
He'd heard from Melora's children all about
aeroplanes, about school and some of the other
differences in the country he'd be going to.

'I'm scared,' he said in English, and Cora gathered him into her arms and held him tight.

She knew at the age of three that he would
barely remember this experience in future years
and that now was indeed the right time to effect
these changes in his life. Travelling between the
two countries would become second nature to
him, just as it had for Melora and Daniel's children.

'I will be with you,' she reassured him in Tarparnese. 'I'm your new mother. I'm not going to
let my new son go.'

'My mother?' Nee-Ty looked at her as though

realising this for the first time. Granted, the last few weeks had been filled with new experiences for him. He'd laughed and played with the other children, both Australian and Tarparniian, and he'd fallen asleep every night between Archer and herself. '*My* mother?' There was slight desperation in his tone and Cora instantly hugged him closer, wanting him to feel the love she gave freely.

'Yes, my son.'

'I can call you Mother?'

'Yes.' There were tears in her eyes and a lump in her throat as she nodded. 'I am your mother.'

He pulled back and looked at her, placing his little hands on either side of her face. 'My mother?' Again, his words seemed incredulous, as though he'd never thought this new life of his was ever a possibility.

'Yes, my son.' Cora sniffed and pressed kisses to his gorgeous face. 'I love you.'

Nee-Ty threw his arms around her neck and hugged her so tight she thought he might never let her go again. '*My mother.*' He was still for a whole two seconds before he eased back, settling in her arms with such confidence, as though he knew she would always adjust her position, her hold on him to ensure he never fell.

When it was time for them to leave the village, Nahkala told Nee-Ty that she would see him again, that he was always welcome here, that this was now his ancestral home and that she, as matriarch, held his mask for safekeeping. Nee-Ty, because he'd been raised to understand these rituals, accepted her words.

'I'm so glad you're coming with us,' Cora stated to Archer, as Daniel drove them to the Tarparniian airport in an old army car that had no doors, the seat belt just a piece of rope that fastened across their laps. Nee-Ty was held firmly in Archer's strong arms, clinging to him for dear life.

'First a truck, now a car, next an aeroplane.' She shook her head and smiled at her son. 'I'm proud of you,' she reassured him. His answer was to bury his face in Archer's neck and tighten his grip.

'He'll be fine,' Archer said placatingly.

'Are we doing the right thing?' she asked him, as Daniel brought the car to a stop outside the airport, which was nothing more than a small shed.

Archer held her gaze and nodded. 'Yes. This time will be the hardest for him but that's why we're both here to help.'

'Yes.' Cora sighed and rubbed a hand on Nee-Ty's back, wanting to soothe away his tension. When he saw the aeroplane, he started to cry. She could tell him, until she was red in the face, about the life they would have together in Australia, but none of it meant anything to him.

As they waited for their luggage to be loaded onto the twelve-seater Cessna that would fly them to Sydney Cora tried to calm her son down. The flight wasn't too long but Cora had concerns about how Nee-Ty would take to being cooped up for the duration.

'He'll be fine,' Daniel told her, placing a hand on her shoulder and then one on Archer's. It was only then Cora realised that Archer also had a look of concern about him. 'Kids are resilient. Besides, there are only four other people on the flight so you'll have a bit of room to stretch out. If you can get him off to sleep, it'll be better for him.' Daniel chuckled. 'And you, too.'

Surprisingly, once Nee-Ty was in the aeroplane, with Archer explaining to him everything that was happening, he did seem to settle down. The flight attendant was helpful and brought them a pack of pencils and paper so Nee-Ty could draw and colour in. Even these simple implements were a source of delight to him as he'd only ever drawn in the dirt with a stick. He was amazed at how the pencils were different colours, giggling as he continued to put lines on the paper, continually amazed at the effect.

Archer drew a few pictures for Nee-Ty and that was when Cora realised that the man she'd given her heart to was an amazing artist. 'You're exceptional,' she told him, as she stared at a picture he'd recreated of Nahkala's village.

Archer shrugged off the compliment. 'Something to help Nee-Ty not to feel so homesick. I only wish I could remember the layout of his own village but prior to the cyclone it had been quite a while since I'd been there.'

Nee-Ty was adding his own stripes of colour to Archer's drawing. Cora leaned over and pressed a kiss to Archer's cheek. 'Thank you for coming with me,' she said. 'I don't know what I would have done without you.'

'You would have coped,' he rationalised,

accepting her kisses. He was a man who wasn't used to being loved, used to being cared for, and she'd had a lifetime of both. It was her turn to give to him, to show him just how much he meant to her, without saying the words she knew would probably send him running for the hills.

Cora knew that at some point she'd have to say goodbye to him but thanks to their connection with the little boy they both clearly cared for, their goodbyes wouldn't be for ever. Still, the thought of not being able to see Archer, to chat with him, laugh with him, share with him, kiss him, hug him, watch the small ray of happiness fill his beautiful blue eyes whenever something new and good happened to him…she certainly wasn't looking forward to those times.

She asked no more than he was willing to give but secretly she hoped he'd be willing to open himself up to her completely, to see that it wasn't wrong to unite together, to become a part of a loving and caring family. What she really wanted, though, was to have Archer and Nee-Ty for her *own* family.

As they settled back to enjoy the plane ride, it didn't take long before Nee-Ty was indeed starting to get sleepy. There were four other passengers on the flight, a husband and wife and their teenage son, who sat engrossed in his novel, and a Tarparniian man in his mid-thirties. They'd all smiled politely at each other but for the most part everyone was keeping to themselves. After the strong sense of community Cora had been living with for the past six months, she had the urge to chat with people, find out their stories. For instance, why had the couple and their teenage son been visiting Tarparnii and why was the Tarparniian man on his way to Australia?

With Archer settling back into his seat and the sleeping Nee-Ty quite comfortably lounging all over him, Cora looked at the Tarparniian man, wondering how best to approach him for a chat. Her interest, however, soon changed to one of concern as she noticed he was dabbing sweat from his brow with a handkerchief. With the regulated air-conditioning circulating around the cabin, there was no real reason for the man to be perspiring that much.

Cora peered closer, noting that his movements appeared laborious and lethargic. Was he all right? He tugged at the neckband of his cotton shirt as though needing to find some way of staying cool. He picked up the bottle of water the flight attendant had given to each of them but as he opened it and brought it to his lips, Cora realised he was shaking. Not only that, his breathing was starting to become laboured.

'Uh…Archer.' Cora called softly to him, but he didn't rouse from his doze. She was about to shake him when the Tarparniian man turned his head to glare at her.

'Stop staring,' he ground out in his guttural language.

'You do not look well, friend,' she returned. His eyes widened perceptibly as she spoke his language with a fluency he obviously hadn't been expecting.

'What are they saying?' she heard the woman in the next seat ask her husband.

'Cora?' Archer spoke her name. She turned her attention from the Tarparniian man to look at him. 'Everything all right?'

'I think this gentleman is sick.' She inclined her head to the passenger seated behind Archer and Nee-Ty. Even though she'd spoken to

Archer in English, it was clear the Tarparniian also spoke both languages.

'I am fine.' But even as he said the words he coughed—a weak cough that ended up with him grasping for breath.

Archer shifted Nee-Ty before unbuckling his seat belt and slipping into the vacant seat next to the man. 'I am Archer,' he stated to the man. 'I am a doctor. So is Cora. With your permission, may I examine you?'

'PMA?' the man asked, and when Archer nodded the man almost sagged with relief. Cora asked the flight attendant for the emergency medical kit and quickly located the stethoscope. She handed it to Archer, before checking on Nee-Ty. The child was stretched out over both seats and fast asleep.

'The captain wants to know if we need to make an emergency landing,' the flight attendant said to Cora softly.

'At this stage, I'm not sure. We'll examine him first.' As Cora spoke, she checked through the large emergency medical kit, pleased that it was well stocked and contained a lot of the basic things they might require. From what she could tell simply by looking at the man, either his airway was blocked or there was a problem with his lungs. Either way, the packets of sterile tubing, gauze and needles, among other things, should provide them with whatever they needed. If they needed something that wasn't in the kit, they'd just have to improvise, something she'd become quite adept at during her time in Tarparnii.

'No breath sounds on the left and increased hyper-resonance.'

Cora's eyes widened at this news. 'Pneumothorax?'

Archer looked at the man. 'What's your name?' he asked, and waited while the man took another breath before answering,

'Kon'an.'

'Kon'an, did you get hit in the chest within the last day or so? An accident? A fight?' Kon'an shook his head at Archer's questions. 'Did something fall across you? Across your chest?'

'I have a portable oxygen machine,' the flight attendant offered, and Cora quickly took possession of it.

'Thanks.' Cora gauged Kon'an's rough weight and height and set the dials accordingly. She placed the non-rebreather mask over Kon'an's mouth and nose after he'd told Archer that he'd been trying to fix his car, leaving it for his wife to use, and he'd accidentally hit himself in the chest with the arm of a crowbar while he'd been changing a tyre.

'You've done more damage than you bargained for, and with the pressurisation of the aeroplane cabin it's exacerbated the situation. Your left lung sounds as though it's collapsing.'

'What?' Kon'an was astounded, as were the other people on board.

'We need to lie him flat,' Cora told the flight attendant, and as they reclined the seats, doing the best they could to get Kon'an as supine as possible, the flight attendant once more asked Cora whether they needed to make an emergency landing.

'We're about an hour away from Sydney,' she offered.

'Is there anywhere appropriate we can land that has a good medical facility?' Cora asked, and after the other woman had thought on the question, she shook her head. 'Then we stay on course. Archer and I will do everything we can to help Kon'an.'

What Cora really wanted was an X-ray machine and an operating theatre, but after spending so much time doing 'jungle medicine', as many of the PMA staff termed it, going on instinct was the best way to proceed.

'Can you confirm the diagnosis?' Archer asked, handing her the stethoscope. Cora performed her own examination.

'I concur,' she stated, after listening to Kon'an's lungs. 'The oxygen is ameliorating the air deprivation in the right lung, which is good, but definitely a lung puncture on the left.'

'What's happening?' the wife asked.

'We'll set up to re-inflate the lung,' he stated.

'What's happening?' the wife asked again, and Kon'an looked at Cora, his expression indicating that he, too, wanted to know what was happening.

'Kon'an,' she said, explaining in Tarparnese as she moved in to position near his head.

Archer was seated next to him, pulling different sterile packets from the medical kit. The first thing was an anaesthetic. The sooner they had Kon'an prepped, the sooner they could perform the surgery that would save his life. 'Your left lung is collapsing. You have a small hole in your lung so that when you breathe out, some of that air is going into the pleural cavity, which is between the chest wall and the lung. What we are going to do is to re-inflate your lung so that by the time we land in Sydney you will be all ready to be whisked away to the hospital for further checks and recovery.'

As Cora spoke, the flight attendant translated her words into English for the rest of the passengers.

Kon'an's eyes widened a bit more, fear and terror reflected there now. 'Inflate…my…lung?' he asked, lifting the mask off his mouth and nose so she could understand him better. Cora nodded, placing the mask gently back into place and smiling at him.

'You will do very well,' she told him, still speaking in his native language, wanting to put him as much at ease as possible. 'Archer here has performed this procedure many times and I will assist him.' Cora glanced over at the flight attendant and asked in English, 'Can you get me a paper cup and a fresh bottle of water, please?'

'Uh...sure.' She quickly turned and went to do as she'd been bidden, while Archer administered a local anaesthetic.

'Water?' she heard the wife ask, as though appalled that Cora was thinking about her thirst at a time like this.

'That might make you feel a bit drowsy,' Archer told Kon'an.

'Close your eyes and try to relax,' Cora stated. She pulled on a pair of gloves, Archer having set out everything he would require. She accepted the bottle of water from the flight attendant, quickly opened the lid and tipped a bit out into the cup. Next, she handed the cup to the attendant, before placing the bottle of water onto the floor, hoping they didn't go through any turbulence.

Archer tested to ensure the anaesthetic had

taken effect before glancing up at Cora and nodding. He was about to begin.

Archer made a neat incision into the pleural space. Cora handed him the catheter, which he inserted through the second intercostal space. As he did this, Cora put the other end of the catheter tube into the bottle of water and as the air was removed from the intercostal space via the tube, it exited through the bottle of water, bubbling as it did so.

Archer sutured the tube to the chest wall then covered the wound with an airtight dressing. Cora hooked the stethoscope into her ears and listened to Kon'an's left lung.

'A definite improvement. We'll keep that oxygen in place, though.'

'Good.' He accepted the stethoscope from her and listened for himself, extremely pleased. 'You'll need that tube in for at least the next twenty-four hours but when you arrive at the hospital they'll change the bottle to one with an airtight seal and do X-rays to confirm your lung is re-inflating.'

'The captain has radioed ahead to the airport,'

the flight attendant told them all, speaking in Tarparnese so Kon'an could understand. 'An ambulance will be ready to meet you and take you to the hospital.'

Kon'an tried to nod, to acknowledge her words, but exhaustion and anaesthetic was getting the better of him. Archer performed the man's observations but was pleased with the results.

'He'll pull through,' he told Cora with a confidence she admired. This man made decisions—tough decisions—every day when they were doing clinics, and just as she'd learned, you needed to trust your own judgement.

'I concur.' She smiled at him before leaning over and brushing a kiss to his lips. 'You've done it again. You've saved another person's life.'

Archer tried to smile but it didn't quite reach his eyes. Saving someone's life was easy. Agreeing to meet Cora's family? Opening up his life, his heart, not only to her but to the little boy as well?

Those were all things that threatened his peaceful existence, things that struck him down with fear. He glanced at Cora as she packed up the equipment, his throat growing dry as he wondered how to tell her that he didn't think he could go through with it.

She was relying on him to help her with Nee-Ty but not just now, she wanted him there for the rest of Nee-Ty's life. Could he do that? Was he honestly capable of stepping forward and becoming a father? Due to his own upbringing, he'd vowed never to have children of his own and yet here he was, performing the role of father to a little boy. There was no denying that he cared deeply for the child and would take an interest in his life, but could he really be the man Cora expected him to be?

All he knew was discipline, structure, following orders and making sure everything had a logical outcome. Hadn't he tried to do that, to live that life with Georgie? That had ended in disaster.

Archer wasn't quite sure what Cora saw in him, how she seemed to look at him as though he really was some type of superhero, but he wasn't. He'd told her that from the start. He was just a man. Nothing more, and at the moment, as the plane began its descent into Sydney, Australia, he realised he'd made a grave error.

He wasn't father material. He wasn't husband material and because he cared about both Cora and Nee-Ty, it would be far more beneficial to all of them if he simply extracted himself from the situation as seamlessly and as soon as possible.

CHAPTER ELEVEN

BY THE TIME they arrived at Sydney airport Nee-Ty was still sleeping.

'The whole new adventure thing really has tired him out,' Cora stated, as she lifted the child into her arms. He stirred a little but snuggled instantly into her arms, his head resting on her shoulder.

'It's good that he slept,' was all Archer said as he checked Kon'an's vital signs before the patient was transferred to the paramedics' portable stretcher. Cora glanced at him, realising the brisk military soldier, the man she'd first met, had reappeared. Chances were it was simply because he was now completely out of his comfort zone and, therefore, as he wasn't sure how to act, he fell back on his default setting.

'You saved this guy's life,' one of the paramedics said, as he patted Archer on the back. Kon'an was doing well but there was a look of fear in his eyes as he spoke to Archer in Tarparnese. The man was scared, being sick in a foreign country and not speaking the language too well. She watched as Archer squeezed the man's hand before reassuring him.

Cora felt her stomach churn, listening to Archer tell Kon'an that he wouldn't be alone. She knew it was probably right, that Archer should accompany their patient to the hospital to act as a translator, but at the same time she wanted to remind him that she needed him, too.

'I'll go with Kon'an,' he told her.

'Of course.' She nodded, trying to shift Nee-Ty into a more comfortable position so she could accept the hand luggage from him. 'I'll contact you later.'

'OK.' With that, he turned and walked away from her, heading with the paramedics in the opposite direction from the way she needed to go.

Cora stood there, completely stunned. Archer had literally just ditched her. No *I'm sorry*, no kiss goodbye, he'd just left. She clenched her jaw and tried to ignore the rising panic in her heart as well as the tears beginning to prick at the backs of her eyes. She tried to reassure herself that this was the way he'd behaved when they'd first met, that he'd slipped into military mode because the situation demanded a disciplined approach, but she knew deep down inside that she was lying to herself.

It wasn't what Archer had said, it wasn't that he'd gone to help their patient, it wasn't that he hadn't offered any platitudes when he'd left. It was the fact that his beautiful blue eyes, eyes that had previously warmed her heart, had been cold and distant.

She'd been wondering just how far Archer had been prepared to go with regard to being a father figure for Nee-Ty, and apparently she now had her answer. He'd decided against them. He was sending a clear message that he wasn't someone she could rely on, that he wasn't a superhero after all. He really was just a man…and that was all.

Somehow she managed to pull herself together long enough to collect all their luggage, unsure what to do with Archer's bag, especially as it contained very little. He'd previously told her that he'd buy whatever he needed in Australia as he hadn't had all that much to pack in the first place. By the time she made it through customs, needing to discuss Nee-Ty's temporary visa with them in great detail, she was exhausted.

Where she'd initially hoped that only Stacey and Pierce would make the two-hour drive from Newcastle to Sydney to pick them up, she now wanted to be completely enveloped within the bosom of her family. She wanted to be with people who loved her unconditionally and always would, no matter what. She was now facing life as a single mother and although she knew it would be difficult, she was surrounded by people who supported her. She didn't need Archer after all.

As soon as she saw her crazy family standing there, Lydia and George having made a 'Welcome to Australia' sign, she wasn't able to stop her tears from springing forth. Thankfully, Nee-Ty remained asleep, even though he was a deadweight on her shoulder. Pierce, her brother-in-law, immediately came forward and took the baggage trolley from her, while Stacey wrapped her arms around Cora, being careful not to squash the sleeping child.

'Oh, honey. What's wrong? Where's Archer?'

'Gone.'

'Gone?' Stacey's tone held a hint of disbelief.

'There was a patient on the plane. Emergency.' Cora felt ridiculous that she couldn't stop crying but the emotions she was experiencing were too new and too raw for her to try and control them. 'He's gone to Sydney General.'

'Oh.' Stacey pulled out a tissue and dabbed at Cora's eyes. 'It's all right. He'll be back.'

'No. No, he won't.' Cora leaned her head awkwardly on Stacey's shoulder as she cried. Stacey patted her back, soothing her, but when Nee-Ty began to stir in Cora's arms she instantly forced herself to stop. 'Can't wake him. It's all going to be too much for him.'

'Listen, you're exhausted and Pierce and I were discussing the possibility of staying overnight in Sydney at a hotel, so why don't we do that? You can check in with Archer and get things straightened out.'

'He doesn't want me.' Cora whispered to her sister. 'I saw it in his eyes.'

'Everything all right?' Pierce asked. Stacey shook her head.

'Plan B,' she told her husband.

'OK, everyone,' Pierce said, addressing Cora's siblings as well as Nell, his sister, who lived with them. 'Plan B it is.'

George and Lydia, who were ten and eight, respectively, clapped their hands. 'Yay we get to stay in a hotel overnight.'

'This is the best,' Lydia agreed, and as they all headed off towards the car park Cora couldn't help but completely disagree with her little sister. This wasn't the best at all. In fact, it was the worst.

Archer sat by Kon'an's bedside in the ICU, marvelling at the difference between this sterile atmosphere and the one he'd worked in for the past four years. Most of the time their ICU was a makeshift tent in the middle of nowhere, and while the conditions might not be as sterile, or the equipment as up to date or shiny, the care patients received was second to none. In his humble opinion, that was.

His patient began to stir, finally recovering from the anaesthetic. Upon arrival, the surgeon in charge had decided to take Kon'an to Theatre and insert a proper, more sterile drain.

Archer had waited around, finding the cafeteria and getting himself a much-needed cup of coffee. He'd thought about what he'd done to Cora, his heart aching as he'd recalled the way she'd looked up at him.

It was as though she'd known exactly what he was doing, that he had decided against being part of their lives. How had she known? Did she know him that well? It was true that she probably knew him better than a lot of people, especially given their short acquaintance, but he knew he was doing the right thing. It was better for him to let her down now rather than later. He was not father or husband material. She had to realise that.

Several times he'd wanted to call her, wanted to explain his motives to her, to help her to see that his actions were for the best, but he had no way of contacting her. Apart from his passport and official documents, which were still in his back pocket, he didn't have anything. Where was she? What had she done when he'd literally left her in the lurch?

He wasn't proud of his actions, especially as she would have been left to deal with the bags as well as carry a sleeping child, but by now she'd be once more restored to her family, and hadn't she told him time and time again that she was well supported?

She'd been through a lot, coped with a lot of difficult issues, but now she could move forward with her life, she could be a mother, she could be happy. Of course he knew their paths might cross in the future, especially when she brought Nee-Ty back to Tarparnii, but he hoped that they'd be able to maintain a certain level of professional friendship, if nothing else.

He closed his eyes, grimacing at the thought of nothing else coming his way. He'd have no more kisses from her delectable mouth. No more warmth from her generous hugs. No more laughter from her fast and intelligent wit. She really was the most wonderful woman he'd ever met, and that was why he had to save her from himself.

'Archer?' Kon'an's dry voice pierced his thoughts, and Archer instantly opened his eyes and grabbed the cup of ice chips by the bed. He spooned some into Kon'an's mouth.

'I am here, my friend.'

'My wife. I need to contact my wife. She must learn that I am all right.' His guttural words were tired but filled with urgency.

'I have already begun arranging a message to be sent to her through PMA. You must tell me which village she is in.'

Kon'an gave him the information then eased back into the pillow, resting with a more peaceful expression. 'I was a lonely man,' he told Archer. 'I fought in the war as a young man, seeing and doing things that a teenager should never have had to do.'

'It was a difficult time,' Archer agreed, pleased that Tarparnii was no longer experiencing political unrest.

'I never thought I would live to see a different life and knew that a woman could never love a man like me, with the things I had done.' A smile touched his lips. 'My wife. She is the most wonderful woman. So loving. So accepting. She said my past was my past. I was her future.' He sighed. 'I had never been called a future before. I saw myself differently when I looked through her eyes.'

Archer sat back in his seat, listening to every

word Kon'an was saying and identifying with him one hundred per cent.

'Life is short.' Kon'an's words were slurred as he drifted back off to sleep. Archer's eyes were wide open as he wondered if he hadn't made a grave mistake.

Cora called the hospital to try and get an update on Kon'an's progress. She spoke to the intensive care sister. With her heart beating wildly in her chest, she hesitated before asking whether the other doctor who had come in with Kon'an was around.

'He was here,' the sister replied. 'But I can't see him at the moment. Can I take a message for him?'

Again she hesitated before deciding that she at least had to tell Archer where he could find his luggage, even if he didn't want to talk to her. 'Yes. Thank you,' she told the sister. She left her name and the hotel she was staying at. There. Now the ball was clearly in Archer's court. If he wanted to contact her, he could. If he didn't, well, he may as well just return to Tarparnii and leave her to start her life…her life without him in it.

Even as she disconnected the call her heart started breaking. She threw the cell phone onto the bed before bringing her hands up to cover her face. How could he have just walked away from her like that? Hadn't the time they'd spent together in Tarparnii meant anything to him? The tears started to fall and she didn't want to stop them.

'Cora?' She heard her sister come into the room. 'Oh, my beautiful sister. Is it really that bad?'

'Yes.' Cora dropped her hands from her face and scrambled over the bed for a tissue. 'I love him, Stace. I really love him. With all my heart.' She blew her nose and tossed the tissue towards the bin, missing by a mile. She shook her head and fell onto the bed, the tears continuing to flow.

'I thought I'd finally found a man who was different. He knew I couldn't have children and he didn't judge me for it. Instead, he judged me for wanting to adopt Nee-Ty, but when I explained to him about the accident and how my life was just a miserable ol' mess, he…he kissed me.'

She closed her eyes, remembering that day beneath the large tree with the canopy of leaves. 'He shared things with me, too.' Cora wiped at her eyes and sniffed. 'I thought he was different, Stace. I thought that I could help him to step out from his past into a future that was bright and sunny and had happiness in it. Do you know, he's never really been happy and I thought—' She stopped and shook her head. 'I thought for one crazy moment that perhaps *I* was the one who made him happy. And he's so good with Nee-Ty, even though he didn't think he was, and…and… Why doesn't he want me, Stace? Why?'

The tears came in full swing now and all Stacey could do was to hold her sister tight and offer her another tissue.

'What did he say to you? Did he tell you why?'

'It wasn't what he *said* but how he looked at me. His eyes were all…vacant and closed off. Disciplined. Military.' She almost spat the last word, angry with Archer's father for never having loved his son, especially when Archer was so incredibly easy to love.

'What do you want to do?' Stacey asked, after Cora had blown her nose again.

She shrugged. 'If he hasn't called by morning, I'll leave his luggage with the hotel and we can head home. I need to focus on Nee-Ty. I need to get my priorities straight. I'm a mother now. I have responsibilities.'

'Yes, you do, and your gorgeous new son is busy colouring in with an overly attentive Lydia.'

Cora smiled at this news. Poor Nee-Ty had woken up as Cora had tried to buckle him into the car seat Stacey had provided. The child hadn't liked being restrained and had cried all the way from the airport to their hotel, even though Cora had done her best to try and soothe him.

Once inside their room, though, he'd started to settle down. He'd been mesmerised by the carpet, astonished to find a floor covering that was as soft as a blanket and that he was allowed to walk on it. After they'd opened the adjoining room door, Lydia and George had shown Nee-Ty how to run from one room to the next and back again. Children could always break down barriers with other children, even if they didn't speak the same language.

'It's almost time to get some dinner. Do you feel like going out or staying in?' Stacey asked, even though she already knew the answer. Cora rested her head on her sister's lap, Stacey stroking her back, relaxing her.

'Stay in,' Cora replied. She felt as though she'd been put through the wringer. When Nee-Ty came into the room ten minutes later, he climbed up on the bed and snuggled in next to Cora.

'I think jet-lag might be setting in,' Stacey said. 'Have a sleep. I'm sure everything will settle itself down in time.'

Time. After her accident, her father had told her that her life would settle down in time—and he'd been right. Here she was. Snuggling her son and loving him completely. She should be happy. Her dreams had come true…but in her dreams she hadn't been alone. In her dreams she'd had her handsome hero by her side, the two of them raising their child together. Was it wrong for her to want more? Was it wrong for her to not be satisfied with all the blessings she already had? Was it wrong of her to want Archer, her own handsome superhero, to be by her side for ever and ever?

It must be. Otherwise why would she be hurting so much?

With Kon'an being moved from ICU to the ward, Archer decided it was time he found somewhere to sleep for the night. Before they'd left ICU, though, the nurse had handed him a message that had come in a few hours ago.

It was from Cora, letting him know where they were staying. The instant he'd read it, he'd wanted to rush right over there, to haul her into his arms and to tell her he'd made a mistake, but he knew that would solve nothing.

When he'd left her at the airport he'd sealed his fate. Wrong decisions had dire consequences. His father had taught him that because every time Archer had tried to win his father over, had done something he'd thought his father might like, such as eating breakfast together every morning, the consequences had indeed been dire. His father had rejected him time and time again.

With every wrong decision had come a mental slap about the head, a voice telling him that he was quite useless and to return to boarding school. That his future was bleak and lonely—unless he did as he was told. Marrying Georgie had been a way of trying to gain his father's approval but it still hadn't worked. His father had only shown up at the event long enough to have his press photograph taken with Georgie's father, the two men having sealed the deal on a huge financial merger, before heading overseas.

He'd made the wrong decision with Cora and now it was best if he did return to Tarparnii, just as he'd always returned to boarding school. He stood in the hospital corridor, looking down at the piece of paper in his hand with the name of Cora's hotel written on it. As he had no idea where to stay, he decided that he may as well stay there. He'd get his own room—she wouldn't even have to know he was in the building. Then he'd book a seat on the next plane to leave for Tarparnii and let Cora return to Newcastle to start her new life with her new son.

Fifteen minutes later he was walking into the hotel, pleased they had some rooms available, but even after he was settled in he couldn't help but wonder exactly where Cora was. What room was she in? All he had to do was to call downstairs to the receptionist and ask to be connected to Cora Wilton's room and then he could talk to her.

He picked up the phone, logic demanding he owed her an explanation. He had manners. Military school had drummed that into him with enough drills. Manners cost nothing but were worth everything. He replaced the phone and paced around the room. She wouldn't want to hear from him…would she?

Annoyed with himself for hesitating, he stalked back to the phone and made the call, waiting with an impending sense of doom for the call to be connected at the other end.

'Hello?'

'Cora? It's Archer. We need to talk. I need to tell you why I have to return to Tarparnii tomorrow.'

'Archer? This is Stacey. Cora's sleeping.'

'Oh.' He closed his eyes, feeling like a complete fool.

'But tell me something, because I'm a little confused. Do you or do you not love my sister?'

Archer opened his mouth to tell her it really wasn't any of her business who he loved when he realised that he *was* in love with Cora. He was in love? No. It wasn't possible. He closed his mouth, unsure what he was supposed to say.

'Because if you do,' Stacey continued when he didn't reply, 'then returning to Tarparnii tomorrow is crazy talk. Cora loves you. So does Nee-Ty. Why are you doing this to all three of you?'

Archer was starting to think the same thing. Why was he doing this? Why was he turning away from the possibility of an incredible future with an incredible woman and an incredible boy? 'Uh…I've got to go.' With that, he replaced the receiver then sat down on the bed. Had Stacey just told him that Cora loved him? *Cora loved him*?

His mind whirred with a thousand different thoughts, all travelling at the speed of light, but after what seemed like hours but in reality was about ten minutes he picked up the phone and was once more reconnected with Cora's sister.

'Stacey? I'm sorry about before. I just hadn't realised…something. Listen,' he continued before she could speak or hang up on him, 'I was wondering if you could help me with something.'

'Does it involve you grovelling and apologising to my sister?'

'It does.'

'Oh. In that case, sure. What did you have in mind?'

CHAPTER TWELVE

WHEN CORA AWOKE she felt uncomfortable, grumpy and completely disorientated. She was lying in a bed, a nice big soft bed, but after sleeping on the ground for the past six months, it was difficult to get used to such luxury.

Nee-Ty was lying next to her, curled up, taking up the smallest portion of the bed. She leaned over and kissed him, whispering that she loved him before managing to slide her arm out from beneath him. She shook her arm as she walked around the room, pulling back the closed drapes, trying to remember when she'd drawn them in the first place.

She was quite surprised to find it was daylight outside and when she checked the clock she realised she'd slept for almost ten hours straight. Was it any wonder? Heartbreak combined with jet-lag didn't make for a good combination.

When a knock came at the door, she headed

over to open it, wondering who it could be. She was surprised to see a hotel messenger standing before her.

'Cora Wilton?' he asked.

'Yes.'

'This is for you.' He presented her with a large bouquet of wild flowers before bidding her a polite good morning. With excitement buzzing through her, Cora breathed in the subtle aroma of the flowers before noticing the card.

'"Come to room two-seven-zero,"' she read out loud.

The knock on the adjoining door heralded her sister Jasmine. 'Ooh, what pretty flowers. Who are they from?'

'I don't know. It isn't signed.'

'Oh. Well, check the back. Sometimes people sign the back,' Jasmine suggested, as she took the flowers from Cora and handed her the card.

Cora did as her sister suggested, turning the card over, her heart hammering wildly against her ribs as she saw Archer's name written there. She swallowed, excitement beginning to buzz through her. Archer was here? In the hotel? In room two-seven-zero? He hadn't left? He'd sent her flowers? He wanted to see her?

Suddenly she was having difficulty breathing and she sat down in the chair, fanning her face.

'Cora?' Jasmine eyed her critically. 'Are you all right?'

'Archer.'

'Yeah. What about him?'

'He's here. In the hotel. The flowers are from him.'

'Cool. Well, why don't you go see him and I'll stay and look after Nee-Ty? After all, if Nee-Ty is your son, that makes me his aunty and Aunty Jasmine is definitely brilliant at babysitting.'

Cora looked at her sister for a moment before standing. 'Oh. Right. OK. Well, if you're fine to look after him then I'll—' She stopped, clarity beginning to happen. 'Wait a second. Something strange is going on here. You just happened to turn up right when I needed you and you told me to turn the card over and—'

'Ugh. Stop over thinking and go! Duh. Archer's waiting and you're here yammering on to me.'

'Archer's waiting? He's really waiting?'

'Oh, just go, will you?' The impatient teenager pointed to the door and Cora dutifully pulled on a pair of shoes and headed out to the lift. It took less than a few minutes before she was standing outside room two-seven-zero, and when she raised her hand to knock on the door she couldn't believe just how much she was trembling.

What if it wasn't him? What if Jasmine had got things all wrong? What if—?

But she didn't get the chance to finish that thought as the door was wrenched open to reveal the man of her dreams on the other side.

'Good morning,' he greeted her, sweeping his hand in front of him. 'Please. Do come in. I've been expecting you.'

And it was clear that he had because somehow he'd managed to decorate the room with large plastic trees and plants and flowers. 'Where did you get all this?' she asked, gazing at the room, which looked very much like a fake jungle.

'From a prop store.'

'Of course.' Cora tried not to look at him for too long, tried not to drink her fill, tried not to throw herself into his arms and press her lips to his in a passionate kiss. He really was a sight for sore eyes.

'Why don't you come and sit on the grass over here by the stream?' He took her hand in his, the warmth from his touch instantly spreading up her arm and bursting forth like a million fireworks all exploding at once.

'Wow. Fake grass, a piece of material for the fake stream and even a picnic basket. Is the food plastic?'

'No. The food is real.' Archer helped her to sit down but afterwards didn't remove his hand from hers. Things were definitely starting to look up.

'Oh, before you begin,' she said, 'how's Kon'an? I haven't had the chance to ring for an update.'

'He's doing exceptionally well. In fact, he's been exceptionally helpful too. He made me realise that I was being a complete and utter fool. Why on earth would I give you and Nee-Ty up when I didn't have to?'

'That was my question,' she responded. 'Archer? What happened?'

He looked down at their hands, their fingers

entwined. 'I didn't want to let you down. You were relying on me to help you, not just at the airport—for which I'd like to apologise for my behaviour—but for ever. You wanted me to be involved in Nee-Ty's life, in your life and...' He shook his head, knowing he needed to push through this. 'I'd let my first wife down. She died because of my selfishness.'

'Oh, Archer. How could that be true? You're not selfish.' Cora stroked his arm, so pleased, so happy that he was here, that he was talking to her, that he wasn't giving up on her and Nee-Ty but was actually fighting for them. Still, he had some things to share with her and she didn't want to break his concentration.

'I was back then. For our honeymoon Georgie decided to give me an all-out adventure sports vacation.'

'You went on your honeymoon alone?' Cora's look was quizzical.

'No. Georgie came too. She did everything I did. She parachuted out of a plane. She climbed mountains with me—not the Matterhorn,' he quickly clarified. 'She swam with sharks, she abseiled, she came white-water rafting.' Archer said the last few words slowly. 'Georgie died while we were rafting. She fell out of the boat and although she wore her safety harness, the line snapped and when we pulled her in we discovered she'd hit her head on the rocks and…' He stopped and shook his head.

Cora's heart bled for him, for his pain, for his sadness, for the guilt he'd been carrying around for so many years. 'Oh, Archer. How tragic for you.'

'I've spent the past four years coming to terms with her passing but, still, I can't let anyone take risks just for me, and with you and Nee-Ty I'd be asking you to risk your happiness to be with me. You'd risk everything and I'd let you down.' He shook his head. 'I just couldn't do it. I cared about you both so much that I figured it was better if I removed myself from the equation, to leave you to live your life with the chance of finding happiness.'

She paused for a moment, reflecting on a conversation they'd had at the top of the cliff. 'Is that why you asked me if I'd go white-water rafting again?'

He nodded. 'If I wanted you to go, you said you'd go.' He shook his head. 'I can't do that to you. I don't want you doing anything you don't want to—*just for me.*'

'Because Georgie did. She did it all for you.' Cora's words were a statement, as though she was finally coming to understand him more clearly. 'And you wanted to distance yourself from me so that I wouldn't ever feel obliged to make sacrifices for you.'

'I care about you, Cora.' He lifted her hand to his lips and kissed it, closing his eyes, his words filled with pain. 'I couldn't bear it if I were to lose someone else because of my thoughtlessness.'

'You're not a thoughtless man, Archer. Quite the opposite, in fact.'

'I've forced myself to be. After Georgie's death I made a vow. I promised to devote myself to others, not just in a financial way but in a practical way. Working with PMA, travelling, helping people—'

'Saving their lives,' she interjected.

'With my skills as a surgeon.' He nodded. *'That's* the man I am. The man I need to be. I owe it to Georgie's memory to continue with this work. To be there for my patients. To make a difference where it's needed most.'

'To be a superhero to all…but not a superhero to yourself.' Cora reached over and took both his hands in hers. 'Archer, I think it's incredible what you do and how you devote yourself to helping others, but why is it wrong to find happiness for yourself?'

'Are you saying that I'm not happy?'

'Are you telling me that you are?' She gazed into his eyes, secure in the knowledge that he had feelings for her. He'd said he cared about her—*a lot*. Surely that was a start, right? She waited a moment for him to reply and when he didn't she continued. 'You're an important man in my life, Archer, and not just because of Nee-Ty.' She paused for a moment and took a big breath, unsure whether it was the right time to say something, but, regardless, she was jumping in with both feet.

'I enjoy spending time with you, whether we're helping our patients or climbing a cliff or weathering a storm together. I like chatting with you, learning more about the adventures you've had, the places you've been, the people you've met. And…I'd like more of that.'

Archer shifted uncomfortably but didn't make any attempt to let go of her hands. Cora took that as a positive sign. 'If it was just saving lives that was important to you,' she continued, 'then you could easily get a job in a hospital and use your brilliant surgical skills to continue saving lives, but it's clear that suburbia isn't for you.'

Archer laughed without humour and gave her hands a little squeeze. Cora took that as a sign of encouragement. 'I'm a jungle boy at heart,' he offered, and she nodded.

'I'm aware of that and I also know that if I want to stay near you, to continue spending time with you, then it's going to be…dangerous, and I'm not talking about the adventurous things we might do together.'

'It's dangerous because we care for each other.'

'Yes. I had planned to travel, to see more of the world, but Nee-Ty has changed all that.'

'Yes.'

'His needs must take precedence.'

'Yes,' he agreed.

'But that doesn't mean we have to stay here in suburbia. That's just one plan and if it doesn't work for both of us, even for half a year, then we can come up with a new plan.'

'A new plan?'

She laughed leaned closer and pressed a kiss to his lips. He'd stayed, he'd opened up to her, and she would be forever grateful for his courage in doing that. 'Yes, you stubborn man. Good heavens, you drive me crazy.'

'I do?' he asked softly.

Cora smiled at him. 'Yes.'

'Cora, I've spent all my life following rules. I've never…made up new ones, especially where other people are involved. I can't ask you to give up your family for—'

Cora felt like giving him a swift punch in the nose but instead she leaned forward and silenced him with a kiss. 'Will you shut up?' she asked him softly.

'But—'

'You seem to forget that we met in Tarparnii and that wasn't even my first time there. I've always planned to travel, always wanted to see more of the world, and now I have two special people I can do that with.' She shook her head slowly. 'I don't want to stop the adventure, Archer. I want to keep exploring with you, seeing new things, experiencing new emotions.

'But Nee-Ty?'

She laughed and let go of his hands, spreading her arms wide. 'We can write our own rules, Archer. We can home-school him, teaching him the Western ways as well as the ways of his people. We can hire a tutor to travel with us. In fact, in a few years, once she's finished high school, my sister Jasmine wants to travel. I'd sure be happier if she was travelling with us, at least to begin with, and she'd be able to help with Nee-Ty's schooling. In Tarparnii, when we're working, Nee-Ty can stay with the other village children, just like Melora and Daniel's children do.' There was pure excitement in her tone and she clasped her hands in front of her.

'What do you say?'

'I say you're crazy.' But he was smiling. 'Cora, really, are you sure? I can't ask you to change your life plans just because I feel claustrophobic in normal society.'

'You're not asking me. I'm going to travel, become a permanent member of the Tarparniian medical team, see the sights, climb the mountains and do all sorts of other wonderful things, and I'll still do them even if you choose not to do them with me.' She bit her lip and swallowed the instant sense of panic that engulfed her, hoping he wouldn't simply stand up, thank her for the fun times they'd shared and walk off into the distance without a backward glance. 'But I'd really like you to be by my side,' she added quickly.

'So we can share the experience together?'

'Exactly.'

'And your family? What will they make of all of this? Won't they blame me for whisking you away?'

Cora shook her head. 'My family loves me, Archer. All we can ever want for those we love is for them to be happy. Molly and Stacey know this and so do the younger kids. Jasmine, George and Lydia are going to love Tarparnii. They've always wanted to go and now we have a real excuse to take them. Nahkala's village is now

Nee-Ty's ancestral home. It's important that we not only respect that but embrace it.'

'And you're not doing all this just for me?'

'No. I'm doing it for *us*. You, me and Nee-Ty.'

'We'd be like…a family.'

'A family of our own.'

'My own family.' He shook his head in wonderment then laughed in that rich, deep way she loved. 'My father was wrong.'

'*So* wrong,' Cora added.

'I am family material. I can be a father to Nee-Ty and a husband to you.'

'Husband?'

'Does that scare you?' he asked.

'No. I love you, you crazy man. Why would you talking about being my husband scare me?'

'Well, it scares me,' he admitted on a laugh, then stopped and stared at her. 'You love me?'

It was as though he hadn't realised it could be possible, could ever be true.

'Yes. Why else would I be here?'

Archer drew her close, pressing his mouth to hers, wanting to feel that love, to check that it was real, to check that he really was being granted a second chance at happiness. Cora loved him! How could a man like him be so fortunate as to be blessed twice in love? But this incredible woman was nothing like his princess Georgie. No. Cora was *much* more, in so many ways. He would always love Georgie but she had been his childhood friend. Cora was his equal.

He pulled back, his breathing a little uneven, but thankfully so was hers. 'You *do* love me.' He was certain of it because he'd felt those emotions when she'd kissed him.

'One hundred per cent.' She smiled at him, desperate to hear him say that he loved her too, but there was no way she was forcing him to do anything. He kissed her again, hoping she could feel the way he felt about her, that she knew this wasn't some whim, that he was committed to her, to doing whatever he could to make this crazy relationship of theirs work. They would travel together, making up their own rules, having their own adventures—wasn't loving someone else an adventure? Wasn't taking that huge leap of faith that things would work out, that they could live happily ever after, the biggest adventure of them all? Was he ready for that?

He shifted on the fake grass, bringing his

hands up to cup her face. He gazed down into her eyes, unable to believe just how magnificent she was. 'Cora. My beautiful Cora. I…' He stopped.

'It's OK, Archer. I know how you feel.'

'But I *need* to tell you.'

'Oh. All right, then.' She gazed up at him, keeping her mouth shut.

'Cora Wilton,' he began again. 'My beautiful, crazy, gorgeous Cora. From the first moment I found you, brushed the hair from your face and looked into your hypnotic eyes I began a new adventure. I didn't realise it until just a moment ago. You are…incredible. You're intelligent, giving and extremely caring, always ready to do what's right, and I admire those qualities. I want to learn from those qualities.'

She nodded, not wanting to speak but desperate to kiss him, hold him closer, whisper her love in his ear, but she knew she needed to keep silent.

'I want to spend time with you, travelling, being a family with Nee-Ty. The three of us. A family. And if, in time, we choose to adopt more children, then that's exactly what we're going to do.' He brushed a kiss across her lips. 'Parenting doesn't come from having the same genes. It comes from being bonded in love.'

'Then it doesn't bother you?' she asked, unable to keep quiet when his answer meant so much to her.

'That you can't have children?' He shook his head. 'No. We will love any children we may adopt, just as we love Nee-Ty, because, Cora, honey, I love you.' His words were filled with passion and delight.

Cora sighed, unable to believe how incredible his words made her feel. 'Oh, Archer.' With that, she pressed her lips to his, tears of pure happiness forming behind her eyes. He kissed her back, wanting her to feel just how much he did love her.

It was a while later before they returned to Cora's room, Archer now desperate to see Nee-Ty. The fear at meeting Cora's family had disappeared because now he had a family of his own. Cora loved him and he loved her, and when Nee-Ty saw him the little boy all but hurled himself towards Archer, who instantly let go of Cora's hand so he could gather the three-year-old close.

'You here!' the young boy said in English.

'Yes. I'm here,' Archer answered, and as he put his arm around Cora's shoulders, smiling at her, he leaned over and whispered, 'Let's go meet the family.'

And with a smile the family of three walked further into the hotel room and into their newest and greatest adventure.

EPILOGUE

A FEW DAYS later they were in Newcastle, ready to celebrate their first Christmas together with their new extended family. Archer couldn't believe how instantly welcoming the whole Wilton clan was, and when he met Molly she wrapped her arms about him, hugged him close, before forcing him to dance her around the room.

'And I thought *I* was adventurous.' Cora laughed. 'Even I haven't tried dancing with Archer yet.'

It was also interesting for him to see Cora in her 'natural habitat'. It was clear just how much she loved her family, but he'd realised that the instant she'd wanted to call Stacey the morning after the cyclone had passed.

'Fancy going for a stroll?' she asked him, after they'd cleared away the dishes and leftovers after Christmas lunch. The day had been filled with early morning laughter, opening of presents and a church service before they'd come home to consume an enormous amount of food. All in all, very traditional but not in the way he'd thought. Yes, the plan for the day followed the usual pattern but the honest joy, the spirit of giving, of receiving, of sharing seemed to infect them all.

Nee-Ty had slowly adjusted to his new surroundings and not only was he learning English, soaking it all in like a sponge, he was teaching the other children some Tarparnese. The first few nights he'd slept in the bed with Cora, Archer sleeping on the floor beside them, but last night he'd been intent on sleeping in the spare bed in George's room, more than eager to follow the older boy's lead when it came to the Christmas Day schedule, especially the opening-presents part.

The three-year-old had been flabbergasted at all the gifts, never having received so many things in his short life. 'I hope we haven't spoiled him too much,' Molly had said, after the present frenzy had ended.

Cora had smiled, watching as Nee-Ty played with the remnants of the wrapping paper, his other toys pushed aside. 'I think he can use a little bit of spoiling.'

Now, though, Lydia and George had taken Nee-Ty outside to play with their rabbits, and Jasmine and Nell were going out for a walk to the nearby park. Molly was getting ready to head to the hospital for her shift and Pierce and Stacey had gone to lie down.

'You know, I'd rather stay here,' Archer said, and led her to the lounge, where he pulled her down onto his knee. Cora settled herself onto his lap, snuggling into his warm, firm arms.

'Have I told you today just how much I love you?' he murmured in her ear.

'Yes, but please feel free to tell me again,' she returned, kissing his cheek.

'Have I told you today just how much I need you in my life?'

'Yes, but please feel free to tell me again.' She grinned as she kissed his other cheek.

'Well, have I told you today just how much I want to marry you?'

Cora eased back to look at him, staring at his eyes, checking that he really meant what he was saying. 'Er…no.' It took a moment for her to remember how to speak. 'You did mention something about being my husband a few days ago but, no, no, you haven't mentioned anything about marriage.'

'Oh. Well, please allow me to rectify the matter.' He pressed a kiss to her lips before meeting her gaze. 'My beautiful Cora. I love you, so completely. You keep telling me that I'm your superhero, that I rescued you, but the reality of the situation is that you rescued me. These past few days have been some of the happiest of my life. You, Nee-Ty and the rest of your family have made me feel so accepted. I've never had that before.' He shrugged one shoulder, giving her that gorgeous lopsided smile she adored.

'Yes, my love, you definitely rescued me, helping me not only to live in the world but to really be a part of it because someone I love loves me back.'

He shifted a little on the chair, reaching into his pocket. A moment later he pulled out a ring. It wasn't in a box or a little pouch, just a beautiful ring with diamonds inset into the band. Practical, pretty and perfect. Cora gasped as she stared at it.

'If you don't like it, we can return it,' he stated

'I... I absolutely love it.' She allowed him t
slip it onto her trembling hand.

'Cora, my darling, will you be my *par'machkai*
My wife? My friend, my lover, my helpmate?'

'Yes. Yes, and, yes, to everything else yo
asked. You certainly know how to make a girl'
Christmas wishes come true,' she replied, kiss
ing him with abandon. 'I love you so much,' sh
told him. 'And I hope we can have two ceremo
nies. One here and one in Tarparnii. How doe
that sound?'

Archer smiled and kissed her again, never hap
pier in all his life. 'It sounds like the most per
fect adventure.'

* * * * *

MILLS & BOON®
Large Print Medical

August

A DATE WITH HER VALENTINE DOC	Melanie Milburne
IT HAPPENED IN PARIS...	Robin Gianna
THE SHEIKH DOCTOR'S BRIDE	Meredith Webber
TEMPTATION IN PARADISE	Joanna Neil
A BABY TO HEAL THEIR HEARTS	Kate Hardy
THE SURGEON'S BABY SECRET	Amber McKenzie

September

BABY TWINS TO BIND THEM	Carol Marinelli
THE FIREFIGHTER TO HEAL HER HEART	Annie O'Neil
TORTURED BY HER TOUCH	Dianne Drake
IT HAPPENED IN VEGAS	Amy Ruttan
THE FAMILY SHE NEEDS	Sue MacKay
A FATHER FOR POPPY	Abigail Gordon

October

JUST ONE NIGHT?	Carol Marinelli
MEANT-TO-BE FAMILY	Marion Lennox
THE SOLDIER SHE COULD NEVER FORGET	Tina Beckett
THE DOCTOR'S REDEMPTION	Susan Carlisle
WANTED: PARENTS FOR A BABY!	Laura Iding
HIS PERFECT BRIDE?	Louisa Heaton

MILLS & BOON®
Large Print Medical

November

December

January

0715 LP 2P